THE SPREAD

Book 1 (The Hill)

IAIN ROB WRIGHT

To the good old days. Thank God they're behind me...

"A sickly little smile grew and died on his mouth like a fungus."

China Mieville

"The younger brother must help to pay for the pleasures of the elder."

Jane Austin

"Wherever I wander, wherever I rove; the hills of the highland for ever I love."

Robert Burns

CHAPTER ONE

"Here they come, here they come!" Lightning surged through Ryan Cartwright's veins as a car appeared in the distance, bouncing up the hillside. The lads were over three hours late, but that didn't matter. They were here now.

This is gonna be legendary. No women. No work. No worries.

Disappointingly, Ryan's younger brother, Aaron, didn't even feign excitement. It had taken weeks of hard persuasion to get him to leave his video games behind for a couple of days, but he was making no effort to disguise the fact he didn't want to be there.

Pasty-skinned and greasy-haired, Aaron looked very little like Ryan – and the differences continued beyond appearances. While Ryan was confident and athletic, Aaron was a loner who would benefit from a little more sun. Besides having the same chestnut brown hair and matching green eyes, they looked completely unrelated. All the same, Ryan was glad his little brother had come along on this weekend – it meant a lot – so he put an arm around him and gave a reassuring squeeze. "It'll be a laugh, I promise."

Aaron nodded. "Yeah."

The approaching car was a sleek four-by-four, and in the weak Autumnal sunshine its opulent red paint shone like a thousand rubies. It crunched to a halt on the weedy gravel in front of the cottage, completely out of place against the ancient landscape. The engine grumbled and the vehicle went to sleep. All four of its doors opened.

Ryan met Tom at the driver's side. His friend's neat blonde hair had grown long, and a fuzzy goatee elongated his slender face. "Nice motor, mate. What is it?"

Tom grinned proudly, running a hand over the sleek red bonnet. "Alfa Romeo Stelvio. Drove it away from the dealership last week as a treat for having such a great financial year. Handsome, isn't she? I'm actually considering breaking things off with Amanda just so I can spend more time behind the wheel. Would that be incredibly materialistic of me?"

Ryan chuckled. "I reckon so, yeah, mate. How are things going with Amanda, anyway? It's been six months and you haven't even introduced us yet."

"I'm cautiously optimistic that she may be the one. We'll have to grab dinner together soon."

"I'd like that."

Loobey rounded the Stelvio's bonnet, his belly jiggling beneath a stripy jumper. A grin took up most of his face. "She didn't run a mile when she saw Tom's tiny knob, so that's a good sign."

Tom rolled his eyes but took the joke as intended. "I wanted to call her, actually, to let her know we've arrived safely, but I haven't had a signal since we left the village. Is there a landline here?"

Ryan gave an apologetic frown. "Sorry, mate. We're completely cut off out here. No signal. No landline. No Wi-Fi. We can head into the village tomorrow morning, though, to make a call, if that's cool?"

Tom seemed to mull it over, both hands in his chino pockets. He was the only one of them not wearing jeans. "Hmm, I suppose that'll have to be okay. Hopefully she won't worry too much."

"Treat 'em mean, keep 'em keen," said Loobey. "It'll only make her want you more."

Ryan gave his best friend a hug. "How you doing, Loobey? I ain't seen you, man! Where you been hiding?"

"Been proper busy, mate. Old man got a job tarmacking for the council and it's been a right mad'un."

"Well, at least you've got plenty of work. You look like you've lost weight."

Loobey put his hands on his hips and gyrated. "Ain't morbidly obese no more, me, just regular obese. Lasses can't get enough."

Ryan chuckled. "I'll bet."

Loobey definitely looked better for the weight loss, but something about him didn't seem quite right. It was as if his bones were too big for his body. He'd shaved his head as well, which made his face appear pudgy and round.

Might have to break it to you later, our kid. It's not a good look.

Sean and Brett moved from the rear of the Stelvio and joined everyone at the front. Sean was twitching like a maniac, as per usual, the human incarnation of '*mad fer it*'. His green eyes shifted left and right as he hopped on the toes of his blood-red trainers. "This place is proper mint. You could chop some poor bastard up here and no one would ever find the pieces."

Next to him, Brett rolled his eyes behind his sensible black glasses. He was always the most serious of the group, but it only took a few drinks to loosen him up. After that, he was as up for a laugh as anybody else. "It's the Scottish Highlands, Sean," he muttered, "not the Nevada Desert."

"There're gangsters everywhere, pal. You should know that."

"Because I'm black?"

"Nah, because you're a shady bastard."

"I'm a fully qualified veterinarian."

"Exactly. What kind of geezer studies eight years to stick his finger up a dog's arse? Shady is what that is."

"Idiot."

Ryan chuckled. He was already having the best time he'd had in ages. Just being with the lads made him happy. When was the last time they'd all been together like this?

Too long. I've been spending too much time with Sophie.

Loobey went to Aaron, who was still standing on the uneven slabs that made up the cottage's front step. "How's it going, our kid?"

"Good."

"You gonna 'ave a lark with us?"

"Yeah."

Loobey didn't push it. He knew Aaron well enough to recognise his shyness, so he tussled the lad's greasy brown hair and turned back to the others. "Sean's right, this place is mint. We're gonna have a right laugh."

"Yeah, we are," said Ryan, looking around and enjoying the scenery with his mates. Living in Manchester, he'd hopped the border into Scotland once or twice, but he'd never gone further than Glasgow. The seven-hour drive it had taken to reach the cottage had been miserable, and at 4 AM this morning, when he and Aaron had set off, it seemed like the biggest mistake ever. That changed as soon as the landlord ferried them up from the village and handed over the keys. Ryan had never seen the sky so wide, or the land so vibrantly hued. He had expected mountainous grey rock and featureless glens, but the Highlands were nothing like that. The land was full of life, coloured in a hundred different shades. A multitude of birds filled the sky. Every bush rustled when you passed it, unseen critters hiding within. The drive had been worth it.

This entire weekend will be worth it.

"Where's your car?" asked Tom, peering around, hands still in his chinos.

Ryan blushed. "I parked up in the village to grab the keys and the landlord pissed himself laughing. Cheeky sod said I wouldn't make it halfway before I ended up in a ditch. I had to leave my car behind while he drove us up here in his Land Rover. McGregor his name was. Could barely understand a word he said."

Sean threw his head back and laughed. "I told yer not to buy that poxy Audi, yer daft bastard. You're a right poser, you are, our kid."

"Hey, don't insult the TT. She's my girl."

Brett folded his arms and raised an eyebrow; his classic pose, born from an innate disapproval of most things. "I thought *Sophie* was your girl. Isn't that why we're all here? To celebrate your love and impending nuptials?"

"Do one!" said Sean. "We're here to get 'angin. Starting now!"

Loobey pulled a face. "Can't we have a mooch first? Let's enjoy some of this clean air. There ain't a kebab shop in sight."

Sean recoiled, orange freckles bunching on his cheeks. "Yer wot? We ain't here to go sightseeing, yer bellend."

"I just want to settle in first before the madness starts. It was a long drive and I'm knackered."

Tom seemed to agree, because he was nodding. "The drive was an endurance test, to say the least. It didn't help that Loobey and Sean were competing in the fart Olympics most of the way here."

Brett grimaced, his glasses rising on the ridge of his scrunched-up nose. "Yeah, that was rough."

Loobey looked away sheepishly. "I couldn't help it. My guts were acting up."

"Heaven's knows why," said Tom. "You didn't eat a thing the entire way here. You must be starving."

"I'll eat later."

Ryan was confused. You could usually depend on Loobey to have a good time, but he seemed on a downer. His reluctance to party was disheartening, but Ryan didn't want to be a dick about it, so he looked at Sean and shrugged. "We're here all weekend, mate. No need to rush."

"Sod that!" Sean reached into his jean pocket and produced a baggie filled with white powder. He dipped a finger in and rubbed the contents on his gums. "Ah, that's banging. Anyone want a taste?"

Everyone declined. While none of them were saints, this was a weekend on the lash, not a re-enactment of *Trainspotting*. Ryan had never been one for drugs – alcohol gave him enough of a buzz. Sean could keep his gear. They still had jobs to go to on Monday.

Don't think about work. That's the last thing I want in my head. I'm here to have a laugh and nothing else. This might be my last chance.

"Okay," said Ryan, clapping his hands together. "Let me give you the grand tour." He strolled towards the side of the cottage, beckoning everyone to follow. "Over here, we have a large, myste-rious shed, which the landlord informs me is to remain locked at all times."

"I'm getting in there," said Sean, "I swear down."

"Try to behave," said Tom, smoothing back his blonde hair as it flapped in the wind. "I know it'll be difficult."

"Sod off."

Ryan glared at Sean playfully. "I had to pay a deposit on this place, mate, so nothing gets broken, okay? It's not even meant for parties usually, but I found it cheap online and convinced the land-lord we'd behave."

Sean pulled a face. "What you mean it's not meant for parties?"

"It's a spiritual retreat or something."

"That would explain the spooky-looking cross over there," said Loobey, pointing to a circle of white stones, within which stood a large wooden cross. The only thing lacking was a sacrificial altar.

"Another thing we're not supposed to mess with," said Ryan. "It's like a hundred years old. The landlord said it would be a crime to damage it."

"I'm climbing it," said Sean, pupils already like dinner plates.

Ryan groaned. "Sean, don't make me regret inviting you, *okay*?"

"I came here to party. It's a stag do, ain't it?"

Ryan rolled his eyes but ended up laughing. Sean was a live wire, sure, but he'd never been any different. A party with him was a party you remembered – and Ryan wanted this to be a weekend none of them ever forgot. "Okay, behind the cottage is a big hill, as you can see. I suggest we don't try to climb it because the nearest hospital is thirty miles away. Back the way we came, down by the road, is a little stream. Me and Aaron have been down there already. It's nice."

"The water's crystal clear," said Aaron meekly. "There are fish in it."

"Skinny-dipping," said Sean, rubbing his hands together. "Nice!"

Brett pulled a face. "Really, Sean? Just us guys?"

"Ryan's got strippers, ain't he?"

Ryan was forced to disappoint them. "You really think a stripper would come out here, two miles from the nearest village, to entertain a bunch of drunken idiots? No way, mate. Would've been a non-starter."

Tom chuckled and gave Sean a playful shove. His expensive watch glittered in the sunlight. "Yes, that would be a rather unwise career move for a young lady."

"We're not rapists," said Loobey, wounded. "Jesus, you make it sound like we're dangerous."

They all looked at Sean.

"One of us has already talked about chopping up bodies," said Brett.

Sean tutted. "I ain't gonna kill nobody, am I? I'm just excited."

"Good to know," said Ryan. "Okay, let's go inside."

"About time!" Loobey clutched himself and shivered. "I'm freezing me nuts off here. You could have booked us a weekend in Ibiza, Ryan."

Sean pinched his belly fat. "Freezing? With all that insulation?"

"Piss off!"

"I'm a bit chilly too," said Aaron, wearing only a light grey jacket. He didn't own anything thicker because he hardly ever left the house.

Ryan nodded to the front door, a solid slab of wood with a cute diamond-shaped window at the top. "Let's get in and build a fire. Everyone, grab yer gear."

They grabbed their bags from the car and headed inside. While the exterior was traditional – white-washed stone and a thatched roof – the interior was modern. Manufactured oak planks covered the floor and the bulk of the living space was open-plan. A compact kitchen-diner adjoined a large lounge area with a fireplace and television. A stack of shiny blue solar panels behind the cottage provided electricity along with a diesel generator beside the shed. Even inside, with the door closed, you could hear the motor thrumming away.

Ryan led everyone to the kitchen counter, which he had stacked full of beers, vodka, and bottled water. There were shopping bags full of snacks on the floor and pizzas in the fridge. "Eat regularly and stay hydrated," he told them, "or you'll be out of the game."

"I'll stick to vodka, me," said Sean, grabbing a bottle and unscrewing the cap. Before he swigged, he looked at everyone and shrugged. "What? It's what we're here for, ain't it?"

Ryan grabbed a beer. "Let's get this party started."

"Because Tom is coming out," said Sean, elbowing Tom in the ribs.

Tom rolled his eyes. "Moron."

Next, Ryan showed everyone to their bedrooms. The master was on the ground floor at the rear of the cottage, through a door beside the stairs. Ryan and Aaron would share its double bed. The staircase was opposite the kitchen, and on the upper floor were three cramped bedrooms. Sean and Loobey agreed to share the room with twin beds, while Brett and Tom had a double each.

Sean pulled a face when they re-emerged onto the landing. "There's only one bathroom? I ain't going in after Loobey's taken a dump."

Everyone chuckled.

"We're in the wilderness," said Aaron. He clutched himself as he spoke, as if he was worried someone might prod him in the chest. "Everywhere's a toilet if you want it to be."

Sean nodded. "Good point, our kid. Loobey, you'll have to drop your kecks outside."

Loobey shoved Sean against the pastel-blue wall. It wasn't a fair fight when it came to weight divisions, but Sean rubbed his elbow and grinned like a Cheshire cat. "Get off, yer fat bastard!"

Everyone laughed. The noise echoed off the old-fashioned white tiles that made up the bathroom's floor. The toilet and bath were lime green, the colour of kiwis. The sink too. Ryan felt a little queasy just looking at it.

Time for an update.

Sean was still beaming. "I've missed you pillocks. We should do this more often."

Ryan nodded enthusiastically. "I know, right? What happened to us? We used to go up town every weekend. Now we're all too busy."

"We grew up," said Tom. "We're not teenagers any more, Ryan. You're about to get married. I'm settled down with Amanda. Loobey has a daughter."

"Brett sticks his fingers up dog's bumholes," Sean added.

Brett rolled his eyes. "You're really on form today, aren't you? Are you going to be like this all weekend?"

"There's a strong possibility."

Ryan sighed, frustrated without really knowing why. "Growing up doesn't mean our lives have to be over though, does it? We can still have a laugh."

"Of course we can," said Loobey. "We're here now, ain't we?"

Ryan patted him on the back. "I'm just missing the old days, I guess."

Sean pointed a finger at Ryan and cackled. "He's getting cold feet, lads! Is that why you dragged us out here in the middle of nowhere, our kid? You running out on the missus?"

Ryan felt himself blush. "Give over. I'm just glad we're all together like old times. It means a lot that you all came."

"Of course we came," said Tom. "We wouldn't have missed it for the world."

"Absolutely," said Loobey, cracking his first actual smile since he'd arrived. "You're my best mates and always will be." Sean reached out and grabbed Loobey's cock, making him shy away. "The hell you doing, Sean?"

"Ah, sorry, our kid. Thought we were gonna start knobbing. Can we go downstairs now and start drinking, you bunch of jessies?"

A smile crept onto Ryan's face. This was going to be a weekend to remember. "Okay, lads, let's go make some memories."

Everyone agreed.

CHAPTER TWO

R yan got a buzz as he started his third beer, and he was pleased to see Aaron moving onto his second. Maybe his younger brother would actually loosen up and have a good time this weekend. That might make it worth the ear-bashing Ryan's mam had given him about taking a fifteen-year-old on a stag do.

Best make sure he doesn't overdo it. A couple of hangovers won't kill him, though. I just need to keep him away from Sean. Yeah, definitely, keep him away from Sean.

A blue three-seater sofa took up the largest part of the lounge, placed opposite the stone fireplace. A beige two-seater sat perpendicular to it, with a black leather armchair completing the U-shaped seating arrangement and a low, glass coffee table making up the centre. A modest television was perched on a table in the corner, while a narrow console table took up the space beside the front door. A lamp and guest book sat on top of it.

Brett was sitting on the larger sofa beside Ryan, sipping from a highball glass full of vodka and coke. As well as being the most serious, he was also the most intelligent – a full-blown vet as of a few months ago when he'd finally qualified. It made Ryan anxious just thinking about the amount of studying and training it must have taken Brett to get to where he was. He would have quit after the first year. In fact, that was what Ryan had done. A year of technical college, but no more, thank you very much. Goodbye forever, classrooms. Stick it up your arse, teachers. Brett was a different animal, though. Driven, determined, and desperate to show that a black kid from Manchester's mean streets could achieve anything an entitled white kid from Hampshire could. To his credit, he had done just that.

Ryan nodded at Brett's drink. "You're off to a good start. Tough week?"

Brett tilted his glass and stared through his glasses into the fizzy brown mixture. "Not particularly. Had to euthanise a four-year-old cocker spaniel, which wasn't fun, but other than that it's been a pretty routine few days."

"I don't think I could do your job, mate."

"After eight years of studying, I would hope not."

"Nah, I mean, I couldn't put an animal down."

Brett tutted. "I'm not a monster. The cocker spaniel ingested rat poison from a neighbour's garden. Its kidneys were failing. It's not my favourite part of the job, admittedly, but I remind myself that animals are going to suffer with or without me. My job is to help those I can."

Ryan raised his pint glass. "Proper respect, mate. I'm proud of you."

Brett clinked his glass against Ryan's. "I'm proud of you too."

"Give over! I'm twenty-five and dig flower beds for a living. Yeah, sure, now and then my boss might let me help lay a deck, but other than that I'm a dogsbody. Right success story, me."

"I'm proud that you're getting married. To be honest, I thought you'd stay a bachelor forever. Instead, you're the first one of us to take the plunge."

Ryan's throat was dry, so he swigged his lager before talking again. "I ain't married yet. This weekend, I'm still a free man."

"I'll toast to that."

"To freedom," said Ryan, loudly enough that everyone heard him.

They all raised their drinks.

"To freedom and drugs," said Sean. In the last two or three hours, he'd taken another two hits from his baggie of cocaine, and he was now talking a mile a minute. Loobey had adopted a blank expression, no longer even attempting to keep up. In fact, he seemed liberated by the brief interruption. "Anyone fancy a cuppa?" he asked. "Might take the chill off."

Ryan frowned. "I'm not cold, mate. We've got a good fire going." Thanks to Tom who had stacked the wood like an expert due to having grown up in a big old house that seemed to have an open fireplace in every single room.

"Get a drink down yer," said Sean. "I can't believe you ain't had one yet. What's wrong with yer?"

Loobey shrugged. "I'm just feeling a bit iffy. Think it's travel sickness from the never-ending drive here."

"Excuse me," said Tom pissily. "You were brought here in absolute luxury."

"Your car might be luxurious," said Sean, "but you drive like a joyriding wino."

"If you don't ride an Alfa Romeo fast, you don't deserve to be behind the wheel."

Sean looked at the others while nodding at Tom. "Hark at him. Jeremy sodding Clarkson here."

Tom chuckled. "Yes, okay, Bez."

Everyone hooted with laughter.

Sean straightened up in his armchair. "Fuck's that s'posed to mean?"

"Nothing. It's a joke."

"I don't get it."

"The joke," said Tom, "is that we're all from Manchester, but none of us are anywhere near as Manc as you."

Everyone laughed, except for Sean, who leaned forward with a scowl on his face. His eyes were like deep pools of ink. "I'm proud of my roots, me. Why don't you piss off back to private school if you don't like it, Tom?"

"Whoa, whoa, whoa!" said Loobey. "Chill out, our kid. Don't bring the mood down."

Sean's freckled cheeks flushed, matching the colour of his short coppery hair. "Posh twat and his goddamn Alfa Romeo. Thinks his shit don't stink."

Tom rolled his eyes. "We've been mates for over a decade, Sean. When have I ever acted the snob?"

"You've always thought you were better than us."

Ryan didn't like where this was going. If problems occurred this weekend, it would most definitely be because of Sean; they all knew it. Whenever they had used to go out on the lash, Sean would always be the one to start a fight, or disappear in a taxi with some dodgy bird, but out here, in the middle of nowhere, there were no strangers for Sean to go off on. There were only the six of them.

"Get real, Sean!" Ryan tried to convey the ridiculous of the situation by chuckling as he spoke. "Tom isn't being a snob. He's just proud of his new car. Wouldn't you be?"

"If I worked for it, yeah. Not if my old man bought it."

Tom growled. "Are you kidding me? I paid for it myself. In fact, no I didn't, it's a goddamn lease, okay?"

Sean leapt out of the armchair and started pacing back and forth on the other side of the coffee table like a caged lion. "A lease paid for by a fat solicitor's salary from daddy's firm."

Tom stood up too. "I've had enough of this. More fool me for offering to drive everybody up here. I shouldn't have bothered."

Sean stopped pacing and glared. "You wanna make a move, our kid?"

"No, I do not. I'm going outside to get some air. Please move out of the way."

"And what if I don't?"

Aaron put his hands on his head. "Please, stop fighting."

Ryan leapt up between the two of them. Sean's eyes were all over the place, rolling around like marbles. "Maybe you ought to lay off the powder, Sean. You're being a right dickhead."

Sean rarely got nasty with Ryan, and thankfully this was one of those times. Instead of being outraged, he dropped back down in the armchair and shrugged. "Just having a laugh, ain't I? Calm the fuck down."

"We *are* calm," said Brett. "It's you that's—"

Ryan waved an arm to shut him up. "It's sorted, okay? Let's just have a good time." He pulled a sulky face and stomped his foot. "This is my party and you're ruining it. You're ruining it!"

Everyone howled with laughter. Even Tom, who had sat back down instead of going outside for air. He reached out to reclaim his beer from the coffee table, but it tilted and fell over as the coffee table's glass insert hopped in its metal frame. "What the...?"

A sudden thumping sound – like a condemned Manchester tower block coming down – made everybody flinch. A picture frame, featuring a hairy cow, fell off the wall and smashed against the floorboards. In the kitchenette the oven door swung open. Ryan, still standing, stumbled towards the fireplace, only just managing to grab the stone surround to keep himself from falling into the recently lit fire.

What the hell is happening?

The entire cottage shook, white-painted stone walls creaking. Flecks of ancient paint fell from the uneven ceiling.

"It's a sodding earthquake," said Sean, a mad grin on his face. "Buzzing!"

Brett braced himself against the arm of the sofa. "I've never felt anything like this."

Aaron called out anxiously. "Ryan!"

Ryan stumbled his way towards his brother, trying to keep his balance as the floor rocked beneath his feet. He was utterly confused, and growing more and more terrified as the quaking continued.

Then the quaking stopped.

Everyone looked at one another.

The only sound was Tom's beer dripping over the edge of the coffee table.

After a moment, Tom stood up. "Th-That was rather unexpected."

Sean hopped up, knees like springs. "That was amazing. What a way to remember your stag do, Ryan. A proper earthquake."

Loobey glanced at Brett. "*Was* it an earthquake?"

Brett shrugged. "I suppose it must have been."

"That was horrible," said Aaron, leaning over his knees and taking deep breaths. "I thought we were gonna die."

Sean patted him on the back and handed him a fresh beer. "Don't let it bother you, little man. It's over now and we can laugh about it."

Aaron took the beer and managed a smile. "Yeah, I suppose it was pretty cool."

"It didn't feel like an earthquake to me," said Tom. "It felt more like... like an impact or something."

Brett folded his arms and frowned. "Like a plane crash?"

"We would have heard an explosion," said Ryan, "but otherwise I agree. It felt like something thumping into the ground outside."

"Maybe it was a boulder falling," said Loobey. "We're surrounded by mountains, right?"

Everyone looked at Brett, causing him to grow irritated. "Why does everyone keep looking at me?"

"Because you're the smart one," said Loobey. "You always have the answers."

"Well, not this time, I'm afraid."

"Let's 'ave a mooch outside," said Sean. "Whatever it was, I wanna see the damage."

"That sounds like a bad idea," said Loobey. "It's getting late."

"You scared of the dark, our kid? Don't worry, I'll hold yer hand."

"I'm not afraid," said Aaron, chest puffed out, "and it would be better to know, right?"

"Absolutely," said Tom. "What if it *was* a boulder and another one falls during the night and crushes us in our sleep?"

Ryan groaned. "I think we might be getting a little carried away here, lads."

"I agree," said Brett. He took his glasses off to rub at his eyes.

"Why don't we just go take a look," said Aaron. "What harm will it do?"

Brett put his glasses back on and shrugged. "I suppose it *is* feeling a little claustrophobic in here. Some fresh air might be nice."

"You lot crack me up," said Sean. "Come on, get yer coats. We're making this party *al fresco*."

———

"I'm freezing," said Loobey, clutching himself inside his grey woollen overcoat.

Ryan frowned. "Really? You look a bit sweaty."

Loobey wiped at his clammy forehead and seemed embarrassed. "*You* try being fat. Temperature control ain't one of my strong points."

Ryan wore a scarf inside his Superdry jacket. He took it off and handed it to Loobey. Truthfully, he wasn't finding it that cold. He'd expected the weather in the Highlands to be biting, but it was only chilly. Having said that, it was September. He could only imagine what December would be like. Would the solar panels around the back even get any sun?

"Maybe it came from up there," said Sean, pointing to the top of the steep hill that rose behind the cottage.

Ryan huffed. "You just want an excuse to climb it."

"It'll give us a cracking view, won't it? If something crashed into the earth nearby, we'll definitely see it from up there."

"He has a point," said Tom.

"No, he doesn't," said Brett. "It's pitch-black. How much of a view do you expect to find?"

"Oh yeah."

"We'd have more of a view than we have down here," said Sean. "I'm going up."

Loobey groaned. "Seriously? I don't fancy climbing."

"Stop blarting. It'll be a piece of piss."

Aaron pointed. "There are plenty of places to get a foothold. It shouldn't be that hard."

Ryan couldn't deny how good it felt to see his brother taking part, but letting him climb a hill drunk felt like a bad idea. The nearby cross made him even more anxious, the white-painted stones reflecting the moonlight and illuminating the ancient wood like a beacon of bad spirits. There seemed nothing holy about it.

What if Aaron falls and breaks his neck? Christ, how would I ever live with myself?

"See you pillocks at the top," said Sean, bolting towards the hill.

"Wait for me," said Aaron, taking off after him.

Ryan called out, "Wait! You slip and fall, and mam will kill me."

"I won't fall, Ryan. It's a fucking hill, not Mount Everest."

Sean howled with laughter. "You tell him, our kid. Stick with me and we'll be up there in no time."

Brett exchanged a glance with Ryan. "You best go with him. I wouldn't leave him alone with—"

"Yeah, no need to finish that sentence. I'm going."

"Fuck me," said Loobey. "Are we really doing this?"

Ryan turned to him. "You can stay down here, mate. Don't worry about it."

"What? And face Sean taking the piss out of me for the rest of the weekend? No thanks. Shite, here I go." Loobey hurried towards the hill, cursing the entire way. "You'll be the bloody death of me one day, Sean."

Tom looked between Brett and Ryan. "He's not wrong. A cracked skull is better than Sean heckling us relentlessly."

Brett looked towards the top of the hill and shrugged. "How hard can it be?"

Ryan sighed. "Come on, then. Let's go kill ourselves."

They all headed for the hill, a loose pack. Aaron and Sean were already ten feet up, racing each other and giggling. Ryan's stomach sloshed with undigested beer as his mind conjured images of his little brother slipping and cartwheeling down the jagged rocks.

The bottom of the slope wasn't so bad, and they were more or less able to walk it, only leaning forward occasionally to keep their balance, but a few feet higher and they would have to crawl. Ryan tried to close the distance on Aaron, wanting to be close by if he slipped.

Please don't slip. Please don't slip.

"Hey," Sean shouted down at them, "after this, we should go looking for magic mushrooms. I bet they grow all over this place."

Brett peered across at Ryan and groaned. "He's a nightmare. You should never have invited him."

"I concur," said Tom.

Ryan put a finger against his lips, telling his friend to keep his voice down. "Shush, he'll kick off if he hears you."

Brett stopped climbing so he could whisper. "So we have to spend the entire weekend on edge, worrying about his temper? He's only just started. He's got enough smack in that baggie to take on a lion."

"Sean would take on a lion sober," said Tom.

"He's our mate."

"That's no excuse, Ryan."

"Look, I'll handle him, okay? Let's just get up this hill. Maybe the exercise will wear him out."

"Like a misbehaving dog?" Brett shook his head and resumed climbing.

They reached the middle of the hill and started using their hands, clambering up like monkeys. Even though it was steep, it was still fairly easy going, the footholds continuing all the way up. Aaron and Sean were near the top, still racing each other. Aaron was winning, which caused Ryan to smile, oddly proud.

He's actually having fun. In fact, so am I. I can't wait to see what's up there. Probably just nothing, but still, there might be—

Ryan made the mistake of looking down, causing moths to take flight in his guts. The solar panels behind the cottage seemed small. They glinted in the moonlight like the surface of a lake, in stark contrast to the cottage's dull thatched roof and white-painted stone. The shed, however, blended into the landscape, a dark shadow against the rocky ground.

Dust blasted Ryan's face, bits scattering in his eyes. He shielded himself with one hand and almost fell. Above him, someone cursed.

"My ankle! It's... I've twisted it!" Brett grunted in a mixture of anger and agony.

Ryan rose up on the rocks, trying to see above and to his right. In the dark, he could see the shape of his hunched-over friend. "Hold on, mate, I'm coming."

"What are you daft bastards doing down there?" Sean shouted from above. "Stop pratting about."

"Just shut up a second," Loobey yelled back. "I think someone's hurt."

Aaron yelled, "Ryan, you all right?"

"I'm fine. It's Brett." Ryan clambered up the rocks and found Brett clutching his ankle. Underneath the moonlight, it was possible to see blood staining his white sports socks. It appeared as a silvery-black stain.

"I got it caught between a pair of rocks," said Brett, hissing in pain. "I don't think it's broken."

"I got you, mate." Ryan put Brett's arm around his neck. "Let's get you down."

"Come on, you lot," Sean shouted. "Little man is about to reach the top. He's mad fer it, this one."

Ryan growled. "Hold on, for God's sake, will you? I'm trying to help Brett."

"I'm coming down to help," shouted Loobey.

"Me too," said Tom. "This was a poor idea from the start."

Sean started to complain. "You lot are a bunch of—"

"Ryan, oh my God." It was Aaron. "Ryan, you need to get up here and see this."

Ryan hissed. "Is anybody listening to me? Brett's hurt and I'm going to—"

Sean shouted and interrupted him, having apparently reached the top with Aaron. "Ryan, you need to listen to your little brother. You need to see this."

Brett glanced at Ryan, his pain seemingly forgotten for a moment. They had both sensed the strangeness in Sean's tone. He had sounded *serious*, which was extremely unlike him.

Brett waved a hand. "Just help me up. I can keep going."

Ryan peered up the hill, trying to see Aaron and Sean, but all he could see was Loobey's arse coming towards him. "Loobey, man, go back up. See what that idiot is shouting about."

"You sure? What about Brett?"

"I'm okay," said Brett. "Just get me up and I'll be right behind you. Don't leave Aaron up there alone with Sean."

"Yeah, okay, mate." Loobey reversed his descent.

"Try not to break an ankle," said Tom sarcastically, which meant he was stressed. He was only ever bitchy when he was under pressure.

Brett rolled his eyes. "Ryan, go kick his posh arse for me."

"Will do." Ryan helped Brett get back upright, making sure he was steady on the rocks, then he resumed his climb, feeling bad about leaving his injured friend slightly behind, but more worried that his younger brother was on top of the hill with only Sean as company. What on earth had they found up there?

Tom was the next to make it to the top, but he didn't add his voice to Sean's or Aaron's, which was worrying. Was he shocked into silence by what he saw? In contrast, Loobey made it up a few minutes later and immediately started shouting. "Holy shit!"

Ryan climbed faster. His guts churned, and he couldn't work out whether it was from excitement or fear. Something was clearly on top of the hill, but he had no idea what. The only way to know was to climb. So that was what he did.

He made it to the top in less than two minutes, hands chafed and scratched from the jagged rocks. His left knee was throbbing. Despite his wounds, he straightened up quickly and found his mates in a huddle, facing away from him.

Ryan limped forward, glad when Aaron turned around and saw him. "Ryan, you need to see this."

"What is it?" He joined the others and got a look at the thing that had captured all of their attention. Again, he asked, "What is it?"

"We have no idea," said Aaron, "but it's cool."

─────

"D'you think this is what caused the earthquake?" asked Loobey, staring down at the strange black object. It was shaped like a spiral – a giant corkscrew. Its black surface appeared metallic and wet, but there had been no rain. Deeply lodged into the ground, it rose six feet into the air before them, widening at the top.

"It must have fallen from a plane," said Tom. "Perhaps from the plane itself, or from some kind of cargo it was carrying."

"It looks like farming equipment to me," said Loobey. He pulled a bottle of water from the deep pocket of his coat and took a swig. "Or an oil drill or something. I bet it weighs a tonne."

"Try ten," said Brett. "It's huge." He had reached the top of the hill and was now limping to join them.

Tom looked around like he expected to see something coming their way, but there was nothing but stars and half a moon. "Perhaps an oil rig exploded. They have a great many of them off the Scottish coast, I understand."

"Yeah," said Sean. "The Jocks are always banging on about their oil. Should've let 'em leave the union if you ask me."

Ryan frowned at Sean. "Seriously? Politics? Now?"

"I reckon it's a secret weapon," said Aaron, his eyes wide and beaming in the moonlight. "Maybe the military launched it as a test."

Tom frowned. "Not much of a weapon. It only managed to knock a picture off the wall."

Aaron shrugged. "Who knows what it does. Could be a radar or something. Maybe it digs into the ground and explodes later."

Everyone exchanged nervous glances.

"Whatever it is," said Tom. "I think we're best off leaving it alone."

"Do we report it?" asked Loobey. "Should we call the police?"

"We'd have to go into the village," said Ryan. He looked at his watch. "It's nearly eleven."

"No one is calling the Old Bill," said Sean. "It's just a chunk of metal in the ground. Look!"

Everyone gasped at what Sean did next. He grabbed a section of the black corkscrew and shoved, locking his jaws tightly as he fought to move it – but it didn't give an inch.

Tom shook his head. "Sean, for Heaven's sake, get down."

"Oh, shut yer gob." Everyone gasped again as Sean leapt up onto the corkscrew, clambering almost to its top. From four feet up, he threw his arms out wide like some coked-up Christ. "See? Nowt to worry about."

Ryan had visions of Sean falling and cracking his skull. That would put an end to the weekend before it even began. "Get down, you idiot."

Sean stopped his frolicking and seemed hurt. He hopped down from the massive corkscrew and tutted. "Why am I the only one trying to have a laugh?"

Ryan sighed. "I just don't want you to get hurt, okay? It's the middle of the night and it's dangerous up here. We don't know what this thing is, so we're best just leaving it alone. I'll tell the landlord about it when we leave here on Sunday."

Sean eyed him suspiciously. "You'll leave it until then? No grassing till the weekend's over?"

Ryan promised. "Like you said, it's just a chunk of metal. It's probably been here for years. We don't even know for sure it's what caused the ground to shake."

"Well, if it isn't," said Aaron, zipping up his light jacket and giving a shudder, "something else caused it."

"I don't even care any more," said Loobey. He was sweating and panting. "I just want to get back indoors in front of that nice warm fire."

"Don't be nesh," said Sean. "It ain't even that cold." He reached out to shove Loobey, but Loobey leapt back and gasped.

"Whoa, what the hell is on your hands, man?"

Sean stopped and raised his palms. They were stained dark by something but appeared silvery when they caught the moonlight. He turned around to face the corkscrew and sneered. "Sodding thing's covered in something. Me 'ands are well rank."

"You can clean off at the cottage," said Ryan. "Come on, let's just get back inside before anyone else gets hurt."

Sean swiped at Loobey again, trying to smear him with the substance on his hands, but Loobey dodged away again, this time only narrowly avoiding the attack. His bottle of water fell on the ground and emptied at his feet, soaking the stony grass. "Get away, man. I don't want that shit on me, okay?"

"It's just oil or something. Don't get your knickers in a twist." He shook his head and tutted. "It's just a bit of oil."

———

Brett's ankle had got worse, leaving him unable to get down the hill unaided, so Ryan and Tom had to carry him. They only narrowly avoided tripping over themselves in several places and were relieved when they finally made it to the bottom safely. Once back inside the cottage, they placed Brett in the armchair and raised his foot up on a stack of beer crates. When Ryan pulled off his friend's trainer, he found an ankle puffed up and swollen.

"Jeez, it's twice the size, mate!"

"It's fine," said Brett.

"It's bleeding. You must have sliced it on the rocks."

"I'm certain it's just a sprain. Do we have any ice for it?"

"Sorry, mate. There's only a tiny freezer, and I filled it with pizzas."

"It's fine. Just get me a drink... and make it strong."

"Coming right up."

Sean was already in the kitchenette, ranting and raving by the sink. Loobey was scrubbing at his hands with a dish scrubber on the end of a stick.

"Just get this shite off me, Loobs."

"I'm trying! It's not coming off."

"Get it off!"

"Calm down!"

Ryan hurried into the kitchen. "What's going on?"

Sean held his hands up to show what was up. His palms were stained dark green with flecks of yellow. Off-hand, Ryan couldn't come up with any idea of what such a substance could be. Instinctively, he took a step back to keep Sean from touching him. "It's not coming off at all?"

Loobey showed Ryan the dish scrubber. Its coarse surface was in tatters. "I got some of it off."

Sean rubbed his hands on his white Armani T-shirt. It was sacrilege, but thankfully the green stains failed to transfer from his hands onto the cotton. "It looks like I've been wanking off the Hulk."

Ryan tried to reassure him. "I don't think there's anything strong enough to permanently stain your skin. Try to chill out."

Sean eyeballed him suspiciously. "What about tattoos and that? They stain forever."

Loobey shook his head. He was leaning over the counter, slightly out of breath and still wearing his coat. "The ink goes underneath the skin, on like the deeper layers or something."

"He's right," Brett shouted from the lounge. "The outer layer of your skin sheds constantly, so nothing can stain it permanently. Not unless it's some kind of dangerous chemical that alters your DNA. Can I have that drink now, please?"

Sean's eyes widened. "Alters my DNA?"

"I'm messing with you," said Brett. "Drink?"

Sean shook his head. "Yer daft bastard, Brett. I'll get you your bloody drink. What you having?"

"Vodka. Neat."

"Think I'll join yer."

Sean fixed a pair of drinks and left Loobey and Ryan alone in the kitchenette. Ryan popped the tab on a fresh beer and offered it to Loobey.

"No, thanks, mate. Reckon I'll get my head down in a minute. Climbing that hill really finished me off."

"Seriously, Loobey, what's wrong with you? This is my stag do and you haven't had one drink. I'm starting to take it personally."

"Well, don't, because it ain't."

"Then what is it? Why aren't you having a laugh with the rest of us?"

Loobey glanced towards the lounge, then back at Ryan. He leaned forward conspiratorially. "Because I've been having chemo, all right? Just keep it to yourself. If Sean finds out..."

Ryan rocked back against the counter, rattling a drawer full of cutlery. The others in the lounge glanced over, but only briefly. They hadn't heard Loobey's confession.

Ryan kept his voice low. "What do you mean, you've been having chemo?"

"Exactly what I said." He ran a hand over his clammy forehead and sighed wearily. "About six months ago, I started getting really tired and weak, you know? Remember, I missed that Man United match with the flu? Next thing I know, I've lost a stone in weight. Then I notice these lumps in my neck. The doctors took some blood tests and samples from the lumps and the results came back wrong. Two weeks later, they tell me I have this thing called Hodgkin's lymphoma. It's rare, but they can treat it."

"They can? So you'll be okay? You're not going to... you know?"

Loobey shrugged, almost like it didn't matter. "What? Am I gonna die? Don't know, mate. They caught it late, which is bad. Normal survival rate is like eighty-five per cent, but I have worse odds than that because I ignored the symptoms for a while. Tell you the truth, I've been feeling exhausted for over a year. I should have got it checked out sooner. Anyway, the chemo has been rough, but the doctors think it's working. It's fine. It's my problem, not yours."

Ryan felt sick to his stomach. "I don't get it, Loobey. How can you have cancer? You're twenty-five."

"I turned twenty-six last month, mate, but it don't matter anyway. Someone has to be the unlucky statistic, don't they? It's fine. I'm dealing with it. Don't tell anyone, okay?"

"They'll wonder why you're not drinking. Is it the chemo?"

Loobey nodded. "Alcohol makes me puke – most things do to be honest. I have some pills to help with the sickness, but I feel rough all the time, mate. Like I said, don't take it personally."

"Jesus, Loobey. I'm so sorry. Is there anything I can do?"

"I just want to take my mind off it for a couple of days. Let's talk about something else, okay? You nervous about the wedding?"

"You could say that. I don't know how I feel about it, really. I know I should be excited. Sophie is amazing, and that, but... I'm head over heels for her, but..."

"But what? What's the problem?"

Ryan blurted it out. "I don't think I want to get married." He placed his fingers against his temples and massaged a circle, closing his eyes. "My head is a mess, mate. I just feel like I'm making this big mistake and that my life will be over. I mean, once I'm married, that's it, right? Next comes kids, a mortgage, working my fingers to the bone."

Loobey struggled for words. "Well, you know... I... shit, man, that's heavy. I mean, sure, marriage will change things – of course it will – but in a good way, right? There's nothing wrong with settling down and having kids. Believe me, I wouldn't change a thing if it meant not having my Lucy. Her mum's a complete nutter and scares me to death, but I look forward to every moment I get to spend with our daughter. It changes you in a good way."

"Does Lucy know you're ill?"

"She's three years old, man. Does Sophie know you're getting cold feet?"

"Of course not. Why the hell would I tell her that?"

"Seems like she's the person you should tell the most. You don't *have* to get married, but I *do* think you have to be honest with Sophie."

"It would break her heart."

"So would marrying someone who doesn't want to get married. Talk to her. Maybe she'll understand."

"How, when I don't even understand myself?"

Loobey reached out and patted Ryan on the shoulder. "You think too much, mate. It's always been your problem. Have you considered that what you're feeling is normal? Marriage is a big commitment; it's supposed to be scary. Life is hard and it never stops moving forward, but you have no choice but to roll with it. Don't you think I wish I could press pause on my cancer for a while so I can catch my breath? Of course I do, but shit ain't like that. I can only try to embrace each day and try not to puke." He grabbed a bottle of water from the counter and let out a lengthy sigh. "Seriously, everything will be okay, but I'm struggling to stand right now. I need to go to bed."

"Of course. Go! I'll tell everyone to keep it down."

"Don't! It's your stag do, man. I'm just sorry that I…"

Ryan hugged his friend. "Don't you dare apologise. You're my best mate, Loobey. I wish you'd told me sooner."

"Me too. I'll see you in the morning."

"Yeah. Good night, Loobs."

Loobey went to bed, leaving Ryan alone in the kitchenette. He looked over at his other friends, all drinking and laughing in the lounge, and didn't know whether to join them. Suddenly, he didn't feel very much like partying.

CHAPTER THREE

"You all right, Ryan?" Brett took his glasses off for a second and rubbed at his eyes. Then he said, "You're a little quiet. This is your stag do, remember?"

Ryan blinked, exiting his thoughts. "Huh? Oh, yeah, I'm fine, mate, just relaxed. Must be the fire."

Brett turned to observe the crackling logs on the metal grate inside the stone fireplace. "Nice, isn't it? I'd love a place like this. Some quiet cottage, removed from all the hustle and bustle, where the nearest bus stop is a few miles away."

"You mean the exact opposite of Manchester?"

"Yeah, I suppose I do. If I never see another red or blue football shirt again, it will be too soon."

"You're joking? I don't think I could ever leave town. It's so full of life – the people, the businesses. Whatever you want, whenever you want it. Out here, it's lovely and that, but I would go out of my mind after a while. I'd have to go into the village every time I wanted to download porn."

Brett chuckled. "You'd have Sophie."

"Oh, yeah. Well, I hope you get a place like this one day, mate. You've worked for it."

Sean leapt up on the other side of the room, a fag in his gob and a bottle of vodka in his right hand. Since Loobey had gone to bed an hour ago, Sean had snorted two lines of coke and drank half the bottle he was holding. He was getting progressively louder, and Ryan wanted to tell him to be quiet, but it would inevitably lead to grief for Loobey. Sean had already kicked off about him going to bed early.

Speaking of Sean, he was currently standing on the small sofa and butchering 'This Charming Man' by The Smiths. Brett pulled a face at Ryan and exhaled. "Here we go again. At least his singing is taking the pain away from my ankle."

"I heard that, yer cheeky bastard. Let's hear you sing."

Brett shook his head, but Sean kept needling him until he relented and sang a couple of verses with him. By the end, Brett was grinning and drinking more readily. His ankle seemed to bother him less and less.

"I hate this song," said Aaron, gulping from his latest beer. He had been joining in more and more as the alcohol sank in, his inhibitions melting away. "Sing something else, Sean."

Sean blasted a finger gun at him. "All right, our kid. This one's for you." He started singing Oasis and everyone was powerless not to join in, making it all the way to the first chorus of 'Wonderwall' before they collapsed in raucous laughter. Ryan felt bad about Loobey, but this could be the last time he got to be with all his mates like this. No way would he waste it.

He'll understand. Some day soon, him and me will laugh about this. We'll celebrate the end of his cancer.

"Oh, I've got one," said Tom, standing up and placing a hand across his diaphragm. He began singing the Verve's 'Lucky Man', even doing an impression of Richard Ashcroft's sullen voice.

"Nah, nah, nah," said Sean. "I hate the sodding Verve. Makes me want to slit me wrists."

"Give over," said Brett, laughing. "They don't sound any different than Oasis."

Sean thrust his hand out with the vodka bottle, sloshing the liquid inside. "Oi! Don't you piss on Manchester's greatest sons."

"Debatable," said Tom. "What about the Buzzcocks?"

"Never mind the sodding Buzzcocks. No band has ever come close to Oasis. The Gallagher brothers are gods. Only the Happy Mondays come anywhere close."

"There's a surprise," said Tom, swigging his beer and chuckling.

Sean glared, a subtle yet detectable darkening of his features. "You and me are gonna fall out, our kid."

"Over music?"

"Yeah, over music."

Tom sighed. "Fine. Let's just agree to disagree."

"Right."

Tom sat back on the sofa and crossed his legs in that feminine way they all teased him about. Perhaps he did it to annoy Sean, but under his breath, he started singing. Slowly, the volume of his voice increased until he was singing the main chorus of '*Bitter Sweet Symphony*' at the top of his lungs.

"Motherfucker!" Sean lunged across the room, vodka bottle raised above his head.

"Shit!" Ryan leapt off the sofa and tackled Sean before he managed to brain their friend. Aaron leapt aside as the half-full bottle bounced off the two-seater sofa and tumbled to the floor, where it quickly vomited its contents. "What the hell are you doing, Sean?"

"He's a sodding nutcase!" Brett was furious, only his swollen ankle keeping him seated. He leaned forward, a furious scowl on his face. "Does he have to ruin everything?"

Sean battled with Ryan on the floor, hurling curse words one after another. Ryan didn't want to hurt him, but Sean's wiry frame made it hard to keep him under control. He kept placing his palms against the floorboards and trying to push himself up, but Ryan did everything he could to keep him pinned.

"Calm the *fuck* down, Sean."

"He's taking the piss. I'm gonna do him. Posh twat."

Ryan grunted, struggling to keep Sean's arms pinned at his sides. "What are you talking about? It's just banter."

"Yeah," Brett shouted. "The hell is wrong with you? You take the piss more than anyone."

"Get the hell off me, Ryan!"

"Calm down and I will."

Sean struggled a little more, then finally went still. "All right, all right, I'm calm. Just get the hell off me before I proper lose it."

Ryan eased up slowly, pausing several times to make sure Sean wasn't faking compliance. Thankfully, he remained calm and didn't fight. Once Ryan was standing, Sean turned onto his side and got up slowly. He was laughing.

"It isn't funny," said Brett. "It's ridiculous. You're a goddamn coke-head."

"It's a sodding stag do. I came to have fun. What is with you lot?"

Brett lifted himself out of the armchair, doing his best to keep the weight off his sprained ankle. Gingerly, he took a step towards Sean, pointing a finger right in his face. "Nobody is doing drugs except for you. The rest of us want to have a good time without acting like maniacs, but instead we're all having to tiptoe around in case you kick off."

"May I also add," said Tom, "that this is the second time you've tried to attack me, Sean. It's getting rather tiresome."

Sean glared at Tom but refrained from doing anything else. He turned to Ryan like a naughty child begging forgiveness. "I'm sorry, our kid. You know me, I'm just having a laugh, ain't I?"

Ryan wanted to let it go. He wanted to go back to drinking and singing and having a good time, but he saw the look on his friend's faces every time Sean got lairy. No one could relax. No one could have a good time. And no way could this go on all weekend.

"We've had enough, Sean. No more coke, okay? You're crazy enough without it, but it's a level of crazy we can cope with. No. More. Coke."

Sean put his hands up, his palms still stained a dark green. "Okay, okay, no more powder, I swear."

"Apologise to Tom."

"What?"

"Apologise to Tom."

"He was trying to wind me up. *He* should apologise to *me*."

Tom tutted. "You'd sooner see Hell freeze over."

"You see? He's got it in for me, the posh twat. I never liked him. Him and that poncey private school. How did he ever end up with us?"

Ryan shook his head, truly disappointed. The five of them had been friends since secondary school. Sure, Tom had gone to a different school than the rest of them, but they had become friends anyway. It helped that Tom's uncle had run a chain of pubs, which meant Tom could get them beer at sixteen – so long as they drank it in the function room out of sight. Tom's uncle made no secret of his dislike for Ryan and the others, but he seemed to realise he was buying friends for his awkward and shy nephew. Truth was, with his posh accent and middle-class manners, none of them would have given Tom a chance otherwise.

But he's one of us. Always has been. What the hell is Sean's problem?

Ryan realised he was grinding his teeth, so he spoke to release the pressure. "I can't believe what I'm hearing, Sean. Tom's a good bloke. You're the one who's out of order."

Sitting on the sofa, Tom had tears in his eyes and was shaking his head in disbelief. "You used to stay at my house, you prick. How many times have you and I gone out drinking together? Now you're saying you never even liked me?"

Sean continued grinning. His pupils were rolling all over the place. Ryan felt like slapping him unconscious. Why was he doing this? Why was he wrecking everything?

He's high as a sodding kite. Even for him, this is extreme.

Ryan studied his friend, taking in the dry skin around his nose and the dark bags beneath his eyes. "Sean, do you have a problem? Do you need help?"

"Give over, I'm fine. It's you lot what has the problem."

Ryan sighed. "Sean, I think... I think maybe we should give you a ride into the village tomorrow so you can catch a train home. We can talk when I get back."

Sean flinched. "Don't be like that, man. I'll stop the blow, all right? Tom, I'm sorry, mate. Of course I like you. We've been mates for donkeys, ain't we? I'm just..." He shook his head and seemed utterly lost for a moment. "Yeah, maybe I am a bit of a mess right now."

"Okay, Sean. I'm glad you can admit that you—"

"I used a different dealer. Reckon he sold me crap. I won't touch any more, right?"

Ryan sighed. He thought Sean had been admitting he had a problem, but it was all down to a bad batch of blow apparently. "Sean, I don't know."

"It's fine," said Tom. "This is your stag do, Ryan. If Sean stops the blow and acts like a normal person for the rest of the weekend, we can all go back to being mates. No one has to leave."

Sean turned to Tom, surprised. "Thanks, mate. No hard feelings, yeah? I was just talking bollocks. Off my head, ain't I?"

"Let's just put it behind us." Tom stood up and went over to Sean, embracing him. Immediately, Ryan felt better. Maybe the weekend could be salvaged.

Still embracing Sean, Tom let out a chuckle. "You're a certifiable nutcase, Sean, but you're our nutcase."

"You fucking wot?" Sean reared back, surprising Tom with the sudden aggression so much that he did nothing as Sean lunged back in and clamped his jaws around his ear.

Tom squealed in pain.

Ryan grabbed Sean and pulled him away, but he kept his jaws clamped, pulling Tom along with them until something tore loose. Ryan was aware of blood in the air and it added to his growing panic, panic that quickly turned into fight instinct. He shoved Sean against the wall in a rage. His friend's skull clonked against the stone and he slumped to the ground.

Immediately, and without any remorse for Sean, Ryan turned to Tom, who was moaning in agony and clutching his ear. Blood ran down his hand and forearm. "Let me see, Tom. Move your hand away."

Tom's hand was shaking as he removed it from his ear, and what Ryan saw was revolting. Sean had torn away the entire lobe, leaving behind a ragged, bloody edge like uncooked steak. Ryan took a step back and felt something beneath his trainer. When he lifted his foot, he saw a morsel of pink flesh crushed against the floorboards.

This is a nightmare and I'm going to wake up.

Suddenly, everyone was shouting and swearing. The smell of blood permeated the air, mixing with the smoky odour of the open fire. Ryan bent over and puked six pints of beer onto the bloody floorboards.

———

It was a good thing Sean was slumped on the ground, because if he'd been standing, everyone would have given him a good hiding. Ryan couldn't believe what his friend had done.

Brett was right. Sean is *an animal.*

Ryan had puked up everything in his stomach, which had the benefit of sobering him up. He sipped from a bottle of water now, staring into space and trying to soothe his scorched throat. Brett was in the kitchenette, cleansing Tom's torn ear over the sink. He'd found a first aid kit in the cupboard and was putting his veterinary skills to use as best he could.

Aaron was sitting next to Loobey on the beige two-seater, telling him about everything that had happened while he'd been asleep. The furore had obviously woken Loobey, but the brief rest seemed to have done him some good at least. He didn't seem so weary.

Ryan heard Sean sobbing in the corner but felt numb as he approached him. "Sean, man, you really messed up."

"I know, I know. My head... I don't know what happened."

"We'll never forgive you for this."

Sean flinched, as if the statement physically hurt him. When he looked up at Ryan, there were tears in his bloodshot eyes. His green-stained hands trembled on his knees. "Ryan, I swear to you, I would never hurt any of you. I would never—"

"But you *have* hurt one of us. You've hurt Tom really bad."

"We should call the police on him," Brett shouted from the kitchenette. "He needs locking up."

Sean nodded. "He's right, man. Call the police. I deserve it."

"We don't have any signal and it's the middle of the night. We'll have to sort this out in the morning. Party's over."

"I hear you. I'll go straight to bed. Can you help me up though? I don't feel right."

"Sure." Ryan offered a hand to Sean and pulled him to his feet, but his friend was groggy and toppled back against the wall. It was then that Ryan noticed the splotch of blood on the stone wall where Sean's head had struck. "Shit, I think I cut your head open when I pushed you. Turn around and let me take a look."

Sean kept a hand on the wall for balance and turned his back on

Ryan. The lump was clearly visible through his short hair, which was bloody in places. "Is it bad?"

"You've got a lump and a cut. I'm really sorry, man."

"Don't be, I had it coming."

"Too right you did," said Brett. He limped angrily into the middle of the lounge. "You're a maniac. Whenever you're involved in anything, it turns to madness. When are you going to get your shit together?"

Sean put a hand up, like he feared Brett might attack him, but Brett had never hit anyone in his life. "Tell me what I can do and I'll do it. What'll make this better? Just tell me, man."

"*Nothing* will make this any better. The damage is done."

Sean looked towards the kitchenette where Tom was leaning over the counter with his ear bandaged up. The way he was taking deep breaths meant he was either in a lot of pain or feeling sick. Probably both. Sean swallowed, a desperate look on his face. "I really fucked up, didn't I?"

Brett turned away in disgust, so Sean looked back at Ryan. "Mate, I'm sorry. I just... I just..." He went to take a step forward, but his left leg buckled and he fell. Ryan grabbed him just in time to direct his fall.

Brett heard the commotion and turned back around. "What's he playing at now?"

"He's hurt," said Ryan, easing Sean onto his side. "He hit his head pretty hard when I shoved him."

Brett's anger evaporated. He knelt beside Sean and started parting the hair at the back of his head so he could inspect the lump. The sight of it made him wince. "He could have a concussion. I didn't see the impact. How hard did he hit the wall?"

"Harder than I meant for him to. I was angry."

"We all were." Brett pulled up Sean's eyelids. He was conscious but lying still and moaning. "We have to get him to a hospital. With all the drugs and alcohol he's taken, a concussion is the last thing he needs."

Ryan cursed beneath his breath. "I can't believe this. Was it always like this?"

"Yes! Why do you think we've been drifting apart, Ryan? This stuff starts getting pretty pathetic at our age. Our crazy days should be behind us. Go tell Tom to get the car started."

Ryan got to his feet, chastised. He went to Tom, who was still leaning over the counter. "Mate, are you okay?"

Tom looked up at him, face pale, lips curled into a snarl in response to his obvious pain. "Oh, I'm wonderful, thank you."

Ryan considered trying to get Tom and Sean to make up, but it would be a selfish act. Tom had the right to never see Sean again if that's what he wanted. "I can't believe he's done this, Tom, and I know it's crazy to even be saying this to you right now, but Sean needs our help. We have to get him to a doctor."

Tom straightened up and his scowl became a frown. "What are you talking about? What's wrong with him?"

Ryan moved aside so that Tom could see into the lounge. "He had a funny turn. Brett's worried he might have a concussion from when I slammed him against the wall."

"Good!"

"Come on, man, you're better than that. With all the blow Sean took, he could end up in real trouble. Do you want it on your conscience if something happens?"

"Seriously, Ryan? Whatever happens to Sean is Sean's fault. Don't place it on me."

"You're right, but that doesn't change the fact we need to get him to a hospital. You could use one yourself. Maybe they can fix your ear."

"Perhaps if you hadn't stepped on it like a clumsy oaf. Brett said there's no way to salvage it."

"Shit! It was an accident. I—"

Tom waved a hand dismissively. "You're not to blame for this."

"I brought you here."

"You *asked* me here, and I was happy to come. There's only one person at fault, and we both know who it is."

As if hearing the accusation, Sean groaned on the lounge floor.

Brett looked towards the kitchenette. "We need to get going, guys."

Tom hissed and shoved himself away from the counter. "Fine, but I'm not stopping at the hospital. I'm going to drive on back to Manchester with anyone who wants to join me.

"You've been drinking," Ryan pointed out.

"Less than the rest of you, and Loobey hasn't had anything, so if he wants to come, he can drive. I'm sorry, Ryan, but I'm going home."

All Ryan had wanted was one last weekend before becoming a fully fledged adult. He had wanted to laugh and joke one last time without a ring on his finger. Sophie was his future, but he wanted to give a proper goodbye to his past. Now it seemed like the past had ended without him realising it. He was trying to recreate something that was already dead and buried.

"I understand. I just hope you can forgive me."

"There's nothing to forgive. I'll go start the car."

Ryan stayed by the counter, suddenly exhausted. He checked his watch and realised it was nearly two o'clock in the morning. By the time they were done at the hospital, he would be a zombie. The last thing he expected to think about this weekend was Sophie, but right now he wanted to lie in her lap while she stroked his hair. The way they did when they watched the *Match of the Day* rerun on a Sunday.

Brett called for Loobey to help get Sean to his feet. When they struggled, Aaron joined them until they eventually succeeded. Sean was wobbly and unable to focus. He kept trying to talk, but only frothy saliva filled his mouth. Ryan grabbed a bottle of water and brought it over. He poured it into Sean's mouth carefully, relieved when he drank some. "You're going to be okay, Sean. We're taking you to a hospital."

"Let's get him outside," said Brett. "The fresh air might wake him up."

Ryan nodded. "Aaron, can you pour some water on the fire? Last thing we need is to come back and find the place in flames."

Aaron rushed off to fill a glass at the sink. Loobey was panting, so Ryan moved him aside and took Sean's weight with Brett. Loobey got the door. Outside, their footsteps crunched on the gravel. The silhouette of Tom's car stood before them, its lights switched off. Why hadn't Tom started it yet?

Tom emerged from the side of the car, dimly illuminated by the light coming from inside the cottage. He jangled his car keys at them angrily. "Who messed with it?"

"What?"

"Someone messed about with my car. It won't start." Ryan reached out to console him, but Tom thrust a finger in his face. "This has gone so far passed the line, Ryan. Who the hell messed with my car? I demand to know right now!"

"No one. Nobody messed with your car."

Tom glared at Sean slumped groggily between them. "It was *him*."

"Didn't," Sean muttered. It was surprising he could even still follow what was being said. "S-S-Swear down."

"I don't believe you," said Tom. "What the hell did you do, Sean?"

Sean's chin was pressed against his chest, but he lifted his head slightly to look at Tom. "D-Didn't."

"We've all been together," said Brett. "Sean hasn't been out of our sight. No one messed with your car, Tom. What's wrong with it, anyway?"

"It's dead. I can't even switch on the dashboard."

"Let me take a look," said Loobey. "Can you lift the bonnet?"

Tom stepped aside grumpily. "Be my guest."

Brett and Ryan stood with Sean while Tom popped the bonnet. Loobey lifted it and propped it up. Then he gave an appreciative whistle. "This is a thing of beauty."

"Yes, I know! Can you see what's wrong with it, please?"

"Hang on. I can't see anything off-hand. The battery's connected. Nothing seems unplugged. I'm no expert, but it all looks fine. You have an alarm, right? It would've gone off if anyone tried to mess with your engine. Yeah, look, the alarm is wired right here. Huh."

"What?" asked Tom. "What is it?"

"Some alarms are connected right to the car battery, which means if it goes flat the alarm won't go off. This one seems to be wired to a backup, though, which means it will definitely go off if someone tries to mess with your engine. There must be some kind of fault. Sorry, mate."

"Impossible. It's less than a month old."

"You'd be surprised. With all the computers onboard, brand new models are just as likely to fail as something older."

"Since when are you a mechanic, Loobey?"

"I've been reading a lot of *Top Gear* magazine lately."

"Wow, then you deserve a diploma."

Ryan pictured Loobey sitting in the hospital all alone, with nothing to do while he waited for his cancer treatment except read magazines from the newsagent. Why hadn't his friend told him about his illness?

I could have been there for him. Hell, I would happily quit my job to attend all of the hospital visits.

Ryan had been planning on leaving his job for a while – digging gardens and laying flagstones stopped being fun pretty quickly – and the thought of getting married had caused him to look at his life through a wider lens. There had to be more to life than poor pay and long hours.

Loobey slipped in behind the Stelvio's steering wheel, the car's suspension rocking gently. It was impossible to see what he was doing in the dark, but he soon returned to join the rest of them. "I can't figure it out. Thing's as flat as a pancake."

"This is outrageous," said Tom, storming back inside the cottage.

"Where are you going?" asked Ryan.

"To get my phone."

"There's no signal."

"Then I'll walk until I get one."

Brett seemed to agree with the idea because he shrugged. "Emergency calls go through on any network. He might catch a signal if he's lucky."

"So we're calling an ambulance now?" Loobey ran a hand over his patchy skull. "This is gonna end up on the local news. *Mancs go crazy in Scottish Highlands.*"

Brett groaned. "Christ, I hope you're wrong."

The door clattered against the wall as Tom came storming back out onto the driveway. "I will seriously strangle someone in a minute."

"What is it now?" Brett demanded.

"My phone's dead too. What is going on here?"

Brett adjusted Sean's weight across his shoulders. "Hold on, I think I have my phone on me." He shuffled a hand into the pocket of his jeans and pulled out a large black phone. He raised it in front of him and thumbed the home button. "Mine's flat too, but it's hardly surprising. It's the middle of the night."

"Mine's plugged in in the bedroom," said Loobey. "You want to go grab it, Tom?"

Tom stormed back into the house while the others waited in tense silence for his return. Out of all of them, Tom was usually the one with the least of a temper. Tonight, it seemed like he might actually strangle someone.

Note to self. Don't get between a posh boy and his toys.

A minute later, Tom returned, still fuming but now appearing slightly anxious. He held up a phone that must have been Loobey's and shook his head. "It's dead. It was on charge... but it's dead."

"The generator's still running," said Ryan. "I can hear it. The lights are on inside."

"Maybe a fuse went," said Loobey. "The sockets might be on a separate circuit to the lights."

Ryan didn't know much about electrics, but he knew how to flip a fuse. He eyed the generator beside the shed. It was rattling away without issue. "That must be it. I'll try and find the fuse box."

Tom folded his arms. "So where does that leave us? We have no phones and no transport. We're two miles from anywhere and it's the middle of the night. Do I go and get help?"

"I don't think anyone should walk off in the dark," said Brett. "I was lucky to only sprain my ankle. It's treacherous on these hills."

"He's right," said Ryan. "You walk about in this dark and you'll break a leg."

"Wanna shleep," said Sean.

Brett let out a lengthy breath. "It's not a good idea to let you sleep, Sean. You might have a concussion."

"Or the idiot has OD'd," said Tom. "This is all his fault."

Loobey was shivering, despite being the only one who was wearing a coat. "Does anyone mind if I go back inside?"

"No," said Ryan. "I think that's what we should all do while we think about this." He looked at Brett to see if he agreed.

Brett gave Loobey a strange look, like he was trying to work something out, but then he turned to Ryan and nodded. "We're going to have to wait this out. We can check the car out properly in the morning and send someone on foot if it still won't start."

Tom fingered at his bandaged ear and sighed. "What about Sean?"

"We'll have to watch him," said Brett. "Any luck and he'll improve."

"And if he doesn't?"

"Then we'll have a lot of explaining to do."

CHAPTER FOUR

Loobey had expected to struggle this weekend, under no illusion that he would feel rotten the entire time. Unable to get hammered with the lads, or even enjoy himself that much, it had been an impossible situation from the get go, but no way had he been willing to miss Ryan's stag do.

Ryan was his best friend and always had been. If not for him, Loobey would have remained the quiet fat kid at school. Large Lewis, the punchline to every joke. Ryan was one of few who never joined in the insults or said anything mean. In fact, Ryan had eventually taken pity on Loobey during his twelfth birthday, intervening when the thugs at their school had been giving him the birthday bumps. Loobey didn't even know how the bullies had found out, because he hadn't told anybody, but Ryan had broken up the ruckus and walked Loobey home. It was the first time he'd felt safe in years.

After that, Ryan had introduced Loobey to Sean, who was two years above them at school. Even then, Sean was crazy, but having him as a friend meant that no one in the entire school dared mess with Loobey ever again. With a little bit of breathing room, he was able to build his confidence and find his feet. Eventually, school hadn't been so bad. You could say it was Sean who had helped Loobey to come out of his shell, but it had all started with Ryan's kindness. No wonder he was the first of them to get married.

People had always loved Ryan – and Sophie most of all. She was a sweet girl from a nice family who never seemed to complain or lose her temper. On the dozen or so occasions Loobey had met Sophie, he had liked her a lot.

But Ryan isn't sure he wants to marry her. Man, that guy doesn't know how lucky he is.

"You sure you're okay to watch him?" Brett asked Loobey as everyone stood inside the cramped bedroom. Sean was lying on one of the twin singles, already asleep. They had agreed to let him nap for an hour at a time before somebody woke him and checked on him. Loobey offered to keep watch until morning.

"I'm fine, mate. I got a nap in earlier, didn't I? Tell you the truth, I ain't been sleeping much through the night lately."

Brett chewed the inside of his cheek, eventually nodding. "All right. If anything happens, you come get me right away, okay? Keep an eye on his breathing."

Loobey waved a hand. "It'll be fine. Get some sleep, you lot. I'll see you in a few hours."

Tom left the room without argument. From the evening he'd had, he probably just wanted to get his head down and be done with things. Brett exited next, leaving behind Ryan and Aaron.

Ryan turned to his younger brother. "Hey, can you leave us alone for a minute, bro?"

"Sure, I'll see you in bed."

"I'll be right along."

Once they were alone, Ryan turned to Loobey. Loobey knew what he would say, so he raised a hand and spoke first. "I'm fine, mate, seriously. I'm going to feel like shit with or without sleep, so it might as well be me who stays awake."

"You need your strength. We don't want to make your... you know?"

"You can say the word *cancer*. It won't upset me. Look, I'll sleep in the morning when you lot sort this mess out. I'm just glad I missed the worst of it."

Ryan nodded, his face a mess of confusion and hurt. It was clear to Loobey how much this weekend had meant to him. "It was rough, Loobs. I still can't believe it happened. Sean needs proper help."

"He's always been an addict," said Loobey, looking down at their sleeping friend. With his eyes closed and still, he was harmless. Innocent. "We can act like it's all his fault, but when did any of us try to help him? We've always laughed at his mad antics and invited him along to every booze-up, but we never once told him to take it easy. I know everyone hates him right now, but I just feel sad, you know?"

Ryan exhaled and seemed to deflate. "My head's a complete mess, Loobey, and I think it's because I feel the exact same way. Despite what Sean did tonight, he's still our mate. In his right mind, he would never want to hurt any of us."

"Problem is, Sean's rarely in his right mind lately."

"Which is why he needs our help. I suppose we'll talk about it tomorrow. You sure you don't mind the rest of us getting our heads down?"

"Nah man, it's sound."

Ryan gave Loobey a hug then left. Loobey collapsed on his bed, gasping for breath. The excitement of the last hour had knocked him for six, but he knew he would be okay in a few minutes. This happened all the time. He just needed to lie still.

Lie still until my body forgets it's dying.

At first, Loobey learning he had cancer had been the scariest thing ever — nothing was scarier than dying, right? — but then he learned that being alive with cancer was even worse. Despite the doctors telling him that his odds of surviving were constantly improving, he had grown weaker and weaker, until he barely felt like himself any more. He was closer to death than ever, even as he fought to live, but it was what lay ahead that worried him most. Health was no longer a straight line, it was a rollercoaster, and he never knew when the next drop was coming. His biggest fear was that he would eventually start fearing life more than death. If that happened, it would all be over. The only light in his life was Lucy, and the thought of leaving her behind caused him even more pain than the cancer.

Three years old. Is that all I get? I want to see her grow old. Fuck, I want to grow old.

It isn't fair.

Sean muttered in his sleep, tormented by a nightmare, or

perhaps remembering his actions from tonight. No matter what happened, Loobey wouldn't turn his back on his friend, and he didn't think Ryan would either. In a way, the three of them were the true heart of the group. As teenagers, their loyalty had always been to each other, but Brett and Tom had held other priorities. Brett had always kept one eye on the future, studying his arse off so he might one day escape. He had always pictured something better – something that most likely didn't involve the rest of them. Tom, on the other hand, had been *born* with something better. As a kid, he would often disappear on month-long summer holidays with his family, or weekends down the races. He had a full life, and his friends were only a small part of it. Loobey, Ryan, and Sean, however, had grown up with little else besides each other. Their bond had been stronger than anything else in their lives.

Until the last couple of years.

Loobey had met Tracey – and welcomed Lucy into the world before realising what a psycho her mam was. Ryan had met Sophie and was about to get married. Brett was a vet, working sixty hours a week. Tom was seeing a lot of Amanda and driving fancy cars. But Sean...

He's been left behind.

Sean was two years older than the rest of them, but was the furthest behind in almost every conceivable way. He'd never been in a long-term relationship, had scarce family, and as for a career; he did the odd shift as a doorman for a couple of Manchester's seedier clubs, but had never possessed anything resembling a steady job. Nothing about his life today was any different today than it had been five years ago – or even ten years ago. The only thing Sean had was his friends, and today he had pushed them away. Loobey's heart ached for Sean, because he was going to wake up to the worst hangover ever.

And he's already had his share of skull-splitting hangovers. Tonight might have been rough, but tomorrow is going to be so much worse.

Loobey turned onto his side to watch his sleeping friend. "You mad bastard. What are we going to do with you?"

Sean mumbled and coughed. It was a wet sound, and if it continued Loobey would have to go and get Brett. Fortunately, Sean returned to silence. His breathing seemed okay.

Loobey began to cry.

———

Loobey didn't know if he'd fallen asleep, but he had dwelled beneath its edges for a while, his dreams entangling with reality. He pictured his cancer growing worse. Coughing and coughing and coughing, over and over again.

But it wasn't him coughing.

Loobey's eyes snapped open and he bolted upright on the bed, still fully clothed in everything bar his coat. He threw his legs over the side of the mattress and saw Sean choking on the other bed. His chest was heaving in and out and his arms and legs were flapping. "Fuck! Sean! Sean, wake up!" He grabbed hold of his friend's shoulder and tried to stop him convulsing. "Shit oh shit oh shit. Brett! Brett, I need you here, man. Brett!"

Thirty seconds later, Brett crashed through the door. "Move aside."

Loobey stumbled away, falling onto his bed. His vision tilted as waves crashed against his stomach lining. He couldn't stop himself from vomiting over the side of the mattress onto the floor. Brett didn't seem to notice.

One by one, the others filed into the room. Ryan saw Loobey lying on his side and probably smelled his vomit. He came rushing over. "Shit, Loobey, are you—"

"I'm fine. Sean needs help."

"Get me some water," Brett yelled, "and towels. He's burning up."

"I'll go get them," said Tom, rushing away. He might have held a grudge, but it was clearly forgotten for the time being.

Aaron stood in the doorway, clutching himself and staring. Loobey put a hand on Ryan's thigh and pushed him weakly away. "Get your little brother out of here, man. He shouldn't see this."

Ryan turned and noticed his brother. Cursing beneath his breath, he quickly ushered Aaron out of the room just as Tom hurried back inside with bottled water and towels. Brett told him to soak the towels, which he did before handing them over.

Brett cooled Sean's forehead. "Sean, Sean, stay with me. Try to breathe for me."

Sean thrashed on the bed, jaws locked together. It was unclear if he could even hear anything being said.

"What can I do?" asked Tom, white as a sheet.

"Help me get his clothes off."

Loobey wanted to help, too, but if he moved, he would be sick again. There was nothing he could do except watch in horror as one of his oldest friends fought for his life. He understood the battle more than anyone else in the room.

You gotta pull through, Sean. There's no giving up. You have to fight.

Sean frothed at the mouth, eyes rolling back in his head. The smell of piss filled the room, mingling with the stench of Loobey's vomit. Brett shook him repeatedly. "Sean! Sean, look at me."

Sean stopped seizing and went still.

"Sean, can you hear me? Sean? Damn it, Sean!" Brett started pawing over his body, checking for a pulse, for breathing, for any signs of life. Loobey wanted to look away, but he couldn't.

I can't do anything to help him.

Brett and Tom ripped off Sean's shirt, then Brett performed chest compressions followed by mouth to mouth. The sound of his palms pumping against Sean's brittle chest was sickening, and Loobey had to take deep breaths not to throw up again. He had spent much of the last few months in hospital, witnessing the fragility of the human body, and he wasn't sure how much more of it he could take.

I came here to escape death. Just one weekend without black clouds hanging over me.

Tom was shaking his head in despair. "Sean, you fool, what have you done?"

Brett switched back and forth between chest compressions and mouth to mouth. Ryan stood in the doorway looking like a ghost, pale skin and mouth hanging wide open. They had failed Sean. They had all stood by and let this happen.

Because we're blokes, and blokes don't nag each other. Blokes don't tell each when they have drug problems or relationship issues. They don't tell each other they have cancer. We stick it out on our own, alone and terrified.

The room fell silent, the only sound that of Brett's palms pumping against Sean's chest. It went on for a full minute, the air turning more and more foul with the stench of piss and sweat. Everyone looked at each other, fear in their eyes. The worst was happening right in front of them.

Then everyone jolted as a giant gasp broke the silence. Tom tumbled off the bed and thudded against the floor as Sean folded in two, chest and knees coming together like two sides of an accordion. He looked around the room, clearly not understanding what was going on. Leaping off the bed, he shoved Brett aside and turned a frantic circle in the middle of the room. "W-What's happening? What's going on?"

Ryan stepped back into the room, speaking calmly despite the fact his nerves were clearly shot to pieces. "Sean, it's okay. You OD'd, but we got you back. Brett got you back."

Sean's hands trembled at his sides. Slowly, he turned to face Brett, fat tears brimming in his eyes. "Am I okay? Am I okay, Brett?"

Brett nodded. "Yes, you're going to be just f..." His words trailed off.

At first, Loobey didn't know what was wrong, but then he saw Sean's naked torso and gasped. "W-What the hell is that?"

Tom was still on the floor, but he scuttled backwards on his hands and feet, clearly horrified.

Brett raised a hand, and placed it before him like he was trying to keep a dog from biting. "Sean, just sit down on the bed for me, okay? Take some deep breaths while I check you over."

Tears ran down Sean's cheeks. "What is it? What's wrong?"

"Nothing is wrong." Brett swallowed and adjusted his glasses with a shaking fingertip. "There's just something on you."

Sean looked at himself, taking a moment before he spotted the strange growths all over his stomach. Patches of green fuzz had sprouted just above his belly button, forming a patchy line that disappeared beneath the waistband of his boxer shorts. A clump of it also covered the back of his right arm. And both hands.

Loobey shifted himself backwards on his bed, pulling his legs up. "What the hell is that stuff?"

Brett shook his head. "I have no idea."

———

Loobey kept his legs tucked up on the bed, wondering if he was delirious from all the chemo. This couldn't be happening, could it?

"What the hell is this?" Sean was pawing at himself frantically and tugging at the tufts of green fuzz covering his body.

"It looks like some kind of fungus," said Brett. "Did you have it before?"

"Before when?"

"Before you got here."

"I've ain't ever seen it before, man. Just get it off me."

Brett leaned forward and examined the tuft on Sean's arm. "Just hold still, okay? Let me take a look."

Sean tried to keep still, but he was trembling. Sweat soaked his face. Loobey felt sweat trickling down his back, but he knew he wasn't an accurate gauge of temperature. It could be freezing in the room for all he could tell.

"It seems to have fused with your skin," said Brett. "I can try to peel it off your arm, but—"

"Do it!" Sean nodded. "Get it off."

"It's the oil," said Aaron, stepping back into the room. Ryan went to remove him, but he dodged and went over to Sean. "Look at the colour – dark green, just like the oil."

Aaron was right. The green stains were all over Sean's hands and sprouting green fuzz. When he moved them next to his stomach, the colour matched exactly. It was all connected.

"What is this stuff?" Sean demanded, starting to panic. "It's a weapon like Aaron said, isn't it? I'm gonna die."

"Stay calm," said Brett. "I still think it's some kind of fungus. There's all kinds of vegetation out here, and we're just a bunch of city boys out of our element."

"I want to see a doctor. Take me to see a doctor, Brett."

"We can't," said Ryan. "Tom's car won't start, and it's too late to walk."

Sean grabbed his face and rocked back and forth with his elbows on his knees. Loobey pushed himself up off his bed, trying to hide how much of an effort it was. He moved over to Sean and put his arms around him, being careful not to let his bare hands touch Sean's sweaty skin. "It'll be okay, mate," he said. "First thing in the morning, we'll get you to a doctor. In the meantime, we're all here for you, okay? Don't be scared."

Sean wrapped his arms around Loobey and Loobey tried not to flinch. Fungus was infectious, right? At least Sean's hands were only making contact with his T-shirt. He swallowed and glanced at Brett. "What do we do now? Is this green stuff dangerous?"

"We have no reason to assume it is," said Brett. "Sean, do you still want me to remove it?"

"Yeah! Get it off me."

"Okay, I'm going to try to pull this patch away from your arm. It'll show us if there's any damage to the underlying tissue."

Loobey held Sean tighter, still keeping his hands raised away from his skin. He turned his head so he could watch Brett work.

Brett asked for the first aid kit and waited while Tom fetched it. Then, he put on a pair of latex gloves and produced a tiny pair of steel scissors. Finally, he got started, snipping at the strange green fuzz and plucking at it progressively harder until the skin on the back of Sean's arm was stretching out like a fleshy tent. "It's not coming off."

"What does that mean, man?" Sean's voice was aquiver. Loobey gave him a reassuring squeeze.

"I'm not sure. Whatever it is, it must produce some kind of bioadhesive. Without the correct solvent, we'd be doing more harm than good by trying to remove it."

Sean pushed Loobey gently away, then stood up and took a deep breath. "I'm going out me head 'ere, lads. What the hell is this stuff? You have no idea, do you, Brett?"

Brett remained sitting on the bed. "No, but that's because I'm a vet and not a doctor. The worst thing we can do right now is panic. Panic helps nothing. First thing in the morning, we're getting out of here, Sean, okay? Until then, we just need to get some rest. You're dehydrated and physically drained, and you've already had one dice with death, so just lie down and try to get some sleep."

"Try to sleep? Are you serious? I'll head out on my own if I have to."

Ryan stepped up to him and got his attention. "Hey, hey, Sean. Let us make the decisions right now, okay? You're not in the best frame of mind."

"Yeah, but Ryan—"

"Look, you know we all care about you, so stop worrying and lie down. We won't let anything bad happen to you."

"You swear?"

"I promise. You're my family, Sean, no matter what."

"I'll be right here with you," said Loobey. "I'll keep an eye on you."

Sean finally seemed to relax. "Okay. Okay, I'll try to rest. I just need some water."

There was a fresh bottle on the bedside cabinet, so Loobey handed it over. "Try to drink it all."

Sean swigged the entire thing down in two gulps. He was out of breath afterwards as he lay down on the bed and stared up at the ceiling.

Brett leaned over, examining him one last time. "We'll get this all sorted out, Sean, okay? Just relax."

Sean reached out and grabbed Brett's wrist. "Thanks, mate."

Brett pulled his arm away. "No problem." Then he quickly exited the room.

"Turn off the light," said Loobey to those still remaining, "and let us get some rest."

Ryan hit the light switch and closed the bedroom door, but before he did, he looked at Loobey, concern written all over his face. Loobey waved a hand to shoo him away, and was relieved when total darkness finally descended upon the room.

He collapsed back on his bed, sick to his stomach and not knowing how he would get through another day without sleep. Constantly tired but unable to rest.

In the dark, Sean spoke. "Loobey?"

"Yeah?"

"I'm scared."

Before he'd been diagnosed with cancer, Loobey had hardly ever cried. Now he did so all the time. Tears slid down the sides of his face now as he stared into the darkness. "Everything will be fine, Sean. Don't worry."

"I love you, Loobey."

"I love you too. Get some sleep."

CHAPTER FIVE

Ryan hadn't slept a wink. He lay in bed, staring at the ancient timber running across the centre of the bedroom ceiling until dawn arrived with a chorus of hundreds of birds. Beside him, Aaron had fared better, passing out the moment his head had hit the pillow. He hadn't drunk much – only two or three beers – but for Aaron it had been a lot.

Mam will kill me if she ever finds out about this. She's never been a fan of Sean as it is.

Ryan's mother had briefly gone out with Sean's dad, years ago, a while after she had left Ryan's father. Sean had been like an older brother back then, babysitting Ryan and teaching him how to play football. When their parents had eventually split – Sean's dad had gone to prison on a GBH charge, Ryan's mother had met Aaron's dad – they drifted apart. A few years later, Ryan started secondary school and discovered that Sean was in a form group two years above. They had quickly rekindled their friendship, Sean once again becoming like a big brother.

He never stopped looking out for me as a kid. He kept Loobey safe, too. Whatever happens, I'll get him the help he needs. He's as much my brother as Aaron.

It wasn't even 6 AM yet, so Ryan had expected to be the first one up, but when he entered the lounge, he found both Tom and

Brett already there. Brett was checking on Tom's ear, his bandaged ankle up on the coffee table.

"Morning," said Ryan, his anxious tummy gurgling as he opened his mouth. "Everything okay?"

"Just eager to be away," said Tom.

Brett rubbed at his hands with alcohol wipes. His glasses were on the coffee table, making his eyes seem oddly small. "I checked on Sean. He's resting, but that green fuzz hasn't gone away. I'm not sure if we try to bring help here or try to take him in the car."

"If it starts," said Tom. "I'll give Alfa a piece of my mind if it doesn't."

Ryan raised an eyebrow. "You don't think one of us messed with it any more?"

"No, I've calmed down and thought about it. Sean lacks a brain, which is why he acts like a Neanderthal. It's not his style to be devious."

Ryan agreed, but just because he hadn't messed with Tom's car didn't mean Sean was off the hook. Not even close. "What he did to you, Tom... he wasn't in his right mind."

Tom ran a hand through his blonde hair, which was blood-stained near his bandaged ear. "I know that, but it changes nothing. He's too unpredictable, and I don't need that kind of stress in my life. Brett and I both agree: Sean is *persona non grata*."

"Let's assume I know what that means," said Ryan. "It sounds like you're writing Sean off just when he needs us the most. He's clearly an addict."

"Clearly," said Tom disdainfully. "He's always been a one-man disaster, but it's up to him how he lives his life. I've never forced him to take drugs or drink himself into a stupor. None of us has."

"We could've done something. Any time in the last ten years, we could have said something to him. Instead, we just laughed along and let him entertain us. He wasn't always this bad. It was a gradual slide that we stood by and watched."

Brett sighed. "Let's just wait for the dust to settle, shall we? If this is Sean's rock bottom – and he actually tries to clean himself up – maybe we'll be there to help him pick up the pieces."

Tom rolled his eyes. "Speak for yourself."

Ryan went into the kitchenette and grabbed a bottle of water.

His throat was like sandpaper, and he finished the entire thing in one gulp, letting out a monumental burp afterwards. "Pardon me."

"Lovely," said Tom.

"Human nature," said Brett. "Better out than in."

Ryan had a rummage. "Hey, there's cereal under the counter if anybody wants some."

"We already grabbed something to eat," said Brett. He motioned to a collection of crisp packets on the table. "We've been up for a while."

Ryan grabbed himself a bowl of cornflakes, his hands trembling slightly, and poured on some milk. Then he grabbed a spoon. With his mouth half-full, he asked a question. "Brett, have you had any thoughts about what the weird fuzz all over Sean could be? It's weird, right?"

Tom tutted. "Knowing Sean, he probably stuck his genitals in something he shouldn't have."

"Come on, man. Give the guy a break."

"Honestly," said Brett, "I still assume it's some kind of fungus, or maybe some kind of bacterial growth. It's not really my area of expertise. None of this is."

"I know," said Ryan. "We're lucky you were here, though."

"Extremely fortunate," said Tom, touching his bandaged ear with his index finger. "I would have gone to pieces without you calming me down and taking charge. I'm not good around blood, especially when it's my own. Remember that time when we were playing football and I cut my knee open on that broken bottle?"

Ryan chuckled, although the situation had actually been quite gruesome. "You went white as a sheet. We had to call your dad to come and get you because you lay on the floor like a plank and refused to get up. Even when he arrived he had to carry you to the car."

"Exactly, and if it weren't for Brett's composure last night, I fear you would have seen a repeat of it."

Brett shrugged. "Dogs, people, it's all the same. Keep them calm and they won't bite you."

"Wonderful, you're comparing me to a dog."

"You're right, I apologise. You're far too prissy to be a dog. You're more of a cat. A Persian Longhair perhaps."

Tom cackled, dimples piercing his cheeks. Tom and Brett had always had a smooth relationship, both even-headed and sensible. In a way, their friendship with Ryan, Sean, and Loobey was an odd fit. If the group ever split, you could be sure that Tom and Brett would end up on the same side.

Something was bothering Ryan, the main cause of his insomnia. "D'you think the fungus came from that metal corkscrew we found on the hill? The oil Sean got on his hands was the same colour as the fuzz on his stomach."

"Seems like the obvious conclusion to make," said Brett. "Metal isn't an ideal breeding ground for fungus, but if it's porous enough, it could allow for growth."

Tom nodded. "My parents had mould on the pipes a few years ago. They had to get half the system replaced."

Ryan gulped down another spoonful of cereal, milk running down his chin. "It was probably antique knowing your parent's house. That place is always falling down."

"That's what you get with Georgian houses, unfortunately. It's on its third roof, and the roots from the poplar trees are starting to unearth the foundations beneath the conservatory. My father has had quite the ordeal."

"I can only imagine the hardship," said Ryan, a forced smile on his face. Tom had grown up very differently to the rest of them, but there was nothing he could do about it, so he had always chosen to own it. Eventually, his poshness had become endearing.

To everyone except Sean, apparently. How long has he been holding a grudge? Or was it just the drugs talking?

"When do you want to leave?" Tom glanced at his expensive watch. "I feel stranded this far from home, and I just want to get back to Amanda. We can crack open a nice bottle of wine while I regale her with courageous tales of how I lost my ear. I'm thinking bear attack. I know they don't exist in Scotland, but fortunately she's not that bright, bless her."

"I want to let Aaron sleep a bit first," said Ryan, "but we'll get going as soon as we can. You sure I can't convince you both to stay, even if Sean gets on a train?"

"I think this weekend is beyond saving," said Tom apologetically. "We'll have to arrange a night out in town, a quiet night with a few beers, perhaps a meal. I'm sorry, Ryan, I know this weekend meant a lot to you."

It did. It meant so much to me, and now it's ruined.

Shit happens, I guess.

Ryan forced a smile. "It's sound, don't worry about it. We'll catch up before the wedding. You're both still going to be there, right?"

"Of course," said Brett, "but I'd think twice about inviting Sean."

"He's my best man. I've known him longer than anyone. Since I was a kid."

"I can't believe you never asked Loobey.

"I spoke to him about it, but we both decided that it would mean a lot to Sean. He's always looked out for me. Loobey too. I owe it to him."

Brett sighed. "Why don't we just try the car and think about getting out of here?"

Tom nodded. "I'm eager to learn whether the wretched thing will start. Come on."

Ryan went to the door. They'd left it unlocked during the night, but it didn't exactly matter out here in the middle of nowhere. All the same, he grabbed the set of keys from where he'd left them upon arrival – on the console beside the door. He didn't want to forget to lock up when they left.

The air that rushed into the cottage when he opened the door was mild, almost humid, and yet the sun outside was barely in the sky. The gravel on the driveway glistened like dewy grass, yet the surrounding grass itself seemed dry. Tom's car was beautiful in the half-light of a morning yet to decide what kind of day it would be. Once again, the Stelvio sparkled like a ruby. Ryan could only imagine driving such a thing, and it made him realise that having four jobs in two years didn't breed success.

I need to find something and stick with it. The problem is, I have no idea what I want to do with my life, and it feels like time is running out.

Brett was standing on one leg, struggling to keep his balance, so Ryan reached out and steadied him. "How's the ankle?"

"Stiff and painful. I didn't sleep a wink."

"Me neither."

Tom raised his key fob and pressed a button. Nothing happened, and he grimaced. "That's not a good sign." Next, he opened the driver's side door, which he had to do manually with the pop-out key. A few moments was all it took for him to reach a verdict. He climbed back out of the car and kicked its tyre. "I can't bloody believe it."

Brett huffed. "It's to be expected. Cars rarely fix themselves miraculously overnight. Okay, well, it looks like someone needs to walk to the village. I would offer to go myself but, um..." He waggled his swollen ankle.

"I'll go," said Ryan. "This is my mess to sort out."

"You should stay with Aaron," said Tom. "I'll go. If I don't call Amanda soon, she'll find another man."

"Sophie will be worrying too," said Ryan.

"I'll call her for you when I get to the village. I... I can't be here when Sean wakes up, okay? I want to be the one to go for a walk. I need to clear my head."

Ryan sighed. "Okay, but please think about forgiving Sean. He didn't mean what he did. He's devastated."

"I just need some time to think."

"I understand. I'm just really sorry that—"

"Just let him think!" Brett snapped. "You can't fix everything all the time, Ryan. You act like it's your job to keep everyone together, but sometimes you just have to let people make their own decisions."

Ryan flinched, but it didn't take him long to nod his understanding. "You're right."

Tom sighed. "I'm going to get going."

There was a shout from inside the cottage, coming from upstairs. It was Loobey.

Brett pinched the bridge of his nose and groaned. "Looks like Sean's awake."

Ryan sighed. "Hold off on that walk, Tom. We might need your help."

Tom groaned. "What is it now?"

"What do you think?" said Brett. "Trouble."

The three of them hurried back inside.

Ryan knew the situation was bad, even before he reached the stairs. A crash sounded upstairs, followed by the sound of Loobey crying out in pain. It could only be Sean. What the hell was he doing?

Aaron was already on the landing when Ryan made it up there, standing unsteadily like a drunken student on Princess Street. When he saw Ryan, he was visibly relieved. "Something's happening."

"It's all right, Aaron. Just stand back, okay?" Ryan moved up to the bedroom door and glanced back to see Brett and Tom standing behind him. Brett had his arm around Tom's neck to keep the weight off his bad leg. His glasses were crooked but he didn't adjust them. Both of them nodded to Ryan, informing him that they had his back.

Ryan shoved the door.

What he saw inside the bedroom was hard to describe. First, there was Loobey, fully clothed and sprawled backwards against a bedside cabinet. Then there was Sean – or a distorted version of him – half-naked and wrestling with Loobey. His face was a picture of pure rage, cheeks the colour of sour milk. Teeth bared.

Ryan threw himself at Sean, not punching or kicking, but using his entire body to remove him. With hands no longer grabbing at his chest, Loobey fell to the floor, gasping. Brett and Tom immediately dragged him out of the room.

Sean had toppled onto his bed, which had become like a pit. The fitted sheet was yellow, dark brown in places, and soaked with piss and sweat. The stench in the room was foul, like the stairwell to a block of flats in a bad part of town.

"Sean, what the hell, man? I don't understand what's happening."

Sean rose to his feet, keeping his back to Ryan. The dawn sunlight came through the window and illuminated him, made his pale flesh seem to glow at the edges. Slowly, he turned around, revealing that his short ginger hair now had patches of dark green in it. The strange fuzz had spread, now covering all of his stomach and parts of his chest.

Ryan gasped.

A floret of green fuzz had replaced Sean's left eye. His other eye seemed confused, half closed with the upper lid flickering. "Ryan? Ryan, I feel well rough. How much gear did I do last night?"

"Sean, just... just sit down on the bed, all right?"

Sean did as he was told, and he did so calmly. The rage that had taken over when he'd been attacking Loobey had completely gone. He spotted a bottle of water lying on the floor and picked it up, drinking from it so ordinarily that it was clear he thought everything was okay. Had he forgotten about having just attacked Loobey?

Sean put the lid back on the bottle of water and dropped it at his feet. He cleared his throat and rubbed at his fuzzy green eye. For a second, it seemed to dawn on him that something wasn't right, but he didn't voice it.

"Sean, you're not well. Why were you trying to hurt Loobey?"

Sean frowned, the question apparently confusing him. "Huh? I was just screwing around, weren't I? I would never hurt Loobey. Shit, I've looked after that kid his entire life."

Ryan nodded. "And you've looked after me too. That's why we're going to get you the help you need, Sean. Someone will walk to the village to get help, okay? In the meantime, you need to stay calm and rest."

In the doorway, Brett and Tom were aghast. No doubt they couldn't believe what they were seeing either. If Sean had contracted some kind of fungus, it was one hell of a specimen. Brett seemed in no rush to study it.

Ryan caught Brett's attention. "Do you know of anything like this? Can fungus do this?"

Brett's mouth remained wide open. All he could do was shake his head.

Ryan stood up. "I'm heading back to the village."

Loobey appeared in the doorway from the landing, covered in sweat and visibly shaken. "No, you need to stay here, Ryan. You're the only one who can handle Sean. He stays calm around you."

The fear in Loobey's eyes gave away the fact he wanted Ryan to stay for his own benefit, too. He was the only one who knew about his cancer. The only one who could cover for him if he got tired or ill.

"He's right, Ryan." Tom adjusted the waistband on his chinos. "Sean sees you as his brother – always has. Without you, he might go nuts, and we won't be able to calm him down like you can."

Ryan turned to Sean. Despite the fact they were talking about him, he showed no recognition of their conversation. He was plucking at a patch of green fuzz on his bony elbow. It was slightly darker than the rest, and crusty.

Ryan gave Tom the nod. "Okay, go."

"I'll be as quick as I can." Tom turned once more, asking Loobey to step aside. Then he disappeared onto the landing.

"Follow the stream," Ryan yelled after him. "You'll find the road a couple of hundred metres down from it."

"Got it!" Tom's footsteps clonked on the stairs.

Brett hobbled into the room with Aaron following. Loobey remained in the doorway, slumped against the frame. Everyone kept their distance from Sean.

Sean smiled, a twinkle in his one eye. "The gang's all here. We gonna party or what?"

Brett folded his arms and tentatively placed some weight on his swollen ankle. "Sean, do you understand what's happening? You've contracted some kind of fungal infection. You need medical attention. You're not in your right mind."

"I'm fine, mate. Hair of the dog and all that. I'll be up for it again in a bit, right as rain. We came here to party, right?"

Ryan shook his head, growing more and more worried by the second. Had the fungus crept into Sean's brain? Why wasn't he panicking about what was happening to him? Why didn't he recognise the dour expressions on the faces of his friends? He looked like something out of a horror movie.

Aaron moved up beside Ryan and whispered, "Is he going to be okay? That stuff is all over him, and it's turning dark in places."

Sean overheard, but he didn't seem concerned. "Stop worrying so much, our kid. Look!"

Ryan jolted backwards as Sean rose from the bed and reached down near the waistband of his boxer shorts. With no reticence, he plucked at a darkening crust around his belly button. It came away easily, making a faint cracking sound as it removed itself. It revealed a patch of clean flesh underneath, but it wasn't healthy human skin. It was milky and smooth, more like bone than meat.

Sean pulled away another chunk of blackened fuzz and revealed another patch of shiny bone. Brett hobbled forward, but he didn't dare grab him. "Sean, stop! You're doing yourself damage." When he failed to listen, Brett snatched at Sean's wrist, even though he clearly didn't want to touch him.

Sean glanced at Brett's hand on his wrist and grunted. For a moment, it seemed like he might get angry, but instead he pulled Brett into a hug. "I love you, man. Stop worrying, okay? I just want to have a good time."

Brett struggled. "Let go of me, Sean."

Sean did not let go. He wrapped his arms around Brett even tighter. Brett struggled and shoved him away forcefully enough that Sean stumbled backwards onto the bed. He was laughing. "Shite, that hurt. Lighten up, man."

"Sean, you need to get some rest. I'll come by to check on you in a bit. We'll bring you something to eat."

Sean went to argue, but Ryan cut in before he could. "We won't be long, Sean, okay? Just chill for a minute."

With a sigh, Sean lay back on his soiled bed, folding his hands over his green stomach. "Make sure you bring us a couple of beers, mate."

"No problem." Ryan turned and ushered everyone out onto the landing. They closed the bedroom door and Brett headed towards the stairs, hopping frantically on his good leg.

"Brett, what's wrong?"

"His hands were all over me, Ryan. Fuck!"

Ryan hurried to catch up with him on the stairs. "You think it's contagious?"

"Yes! It's a fungus. I need to clean myself. Ah, goddamn it!" He winced in pain as he landed heavily on the lower step, jarring his swollen ankle. He almost fell, but Ryan grabbed the back of his shirt and steadied him. "Slow down."

Brett turned aggressively and broke contact. "Don't touch me, you idiot. In fact, nobody touch anybody. Fungus can feed on dead skin cells, which means every goddamn surface in this place could be contaminated."

Ryan's legs felt hollow as he staggered into the lounge and dumped himself on the arm of the main sofa. Aaron came to join him but chose to sit on the armchair. Loobey sat on the bottom step. Brett, however, went hurtling into the kitchen, almost forgetting his injured ankle. He ripped open the cupboards and tore through them. When he found a bottle of bleach, he poured the chemical onto his skin – neat – and started rubbing it all over his hands and forearms. Then he stripped off and rubbed it on his chest and stomach.

Aaron had fear in his eyes, his knee bobbing up and down as he sat and watched Brett. "Won't that burn?"

"I'll take mild chemical burns over a virulent fungus," said Brett, continuing to soak himself with the bleach. "You should all be doing the same."

After a moment's thought, they did just that. There was only a single litre of bleach, so they were forced to dilute it, but Brett told them it was better than nothing. They grabbed a mop bucket they found in a cupboard and filled it with bleach and water before taking off their clothes and scrubbing themselves raw.

Aaron ran his wet hands through his messy brown hair and all over his body until he was shivering with cold. They would need to start a fire to warm themselves up. "Is there a cure?" he asked, his voice fraught with nerves. "For fungus?"

"There are anti-fungal treatments," said Brett. "Most are effective, but... I don't know. Whatever Sean has is something I've never heard about. If we breathe it in, it could take root in our lungs. It could infect our brains."

Aaron wobbled. Ryan grabbed him and made him look at him. "It's okay, little brother. Tom is already on his way to get help. Just stay with me, okay?"

Aaron took a series of shallow breaths, but eventually he gave a nod. "I'm good."

Ryan took a deep breath, trying to keep his heart from beating out of his chest. He turned to Brett. "Sean's confused, like he doesn't even know what's happening. You think the fungus reached his brain?"

"It would explain why he lashed out at Loobey, and why he became so calm afterwards."

"What do you mean?"

"In nature, parasites, fungi, bacteria, and even viruses act to ensure both their survival and their reproduction. If the fungus has got into Sean's brain, it might have caused an initial mood swing or panic that made him attack, but then it rewired his thought processes to keep him calm. If a person doesn't panic, they are less likely to seek help. The longer it takes a patient to see a doctor, the more time the fungus has to take hold. The thing that scares me most is just how *quickly* this thing spreads. The amount of energy an organism would need to grow like that. The fungus must be feeding directly off of Sean's fat cells. The chemical reaction is so fierce that the green fuzz darkens and decays in a matter of hours. We all saw it."

Ryan put a hand over his eyes and shook his head. "This is bad."

Aaron kept the conversation going. "When Sean pulled that patch of dead fuzz away, there was something underneath, as if his skin had turned into some kind of shell."

"I saw it too," said Brett. "Like the surface of an egg. Don't ask me to explain it because I can't. We all need to get a change of clothes and go outside. It's less likely we'll breathe in fungal spores if we get out."

"What about Sean?" asked Loobey. He was still sitting on the bottom step and had been listening to them in silence until now. "He's still our mate, and he's sick."

Brett grabbed a tea towel and started drying himself off. He ignored the question, although he had clearly heard it. He either didn't have an answer, or didn't care to give one. "Okay, that should be enough. Everyone get dry and get dressed. It's all up to Tom now."

CHAPTER SIX

R yan sat on the bank of the stream, watching the crystal water flow from left to right. Now and then a tiny fish would wiggle by, and the carefree movement made the current situation even more surreal.

I'm trapped in a nightmare where all of my friends turn on each other and a fungus is eating Sean.

Aaron sat beside Ryan, poking a bendy stick into the water. He looked nothing like a fifteen-year-old lad from a rough housing estate in Manchester. He was a lost child, which made Ryan feel even more like his father instead of his brother.

That's not my job. It was never supposed to be my job.

Aaron's father had stuck around for the first couple of years after he was born, but eventually the piece of shit had grown tired of being a parent and disappeared to Spain with a friend who had bought a bar. "A once in a lifetime opportunity," he had called it, but it was really just a way to run out on his responsibilities. He might have loved Aaron, but he had no affection for Ryan or his mother. The promises of annual visits had dried up by the time Aaron was six, his father quickly becoming a memory. Ryan had been sixteen and suddenly found himself becoming Aaron's male role model. At the request of their mother, he had tried to include his younger brother in as many things as possible, allowing him to tag along to the few gatherings that didn't involve alcohol or frisky girls. Pretty soon, Sean and Loobey had taken Aaron under their wings, too, but it was hard for a bunch of teenagers to look after a six-year-old responsibly. Aaron was exposed to too much at too young an age, and it scared him. The last straw had been when Aaron witnessed Ryan get beat up after a 'fun time' egging houses.

The egg-based terrorism had been indiscriminate, which somehow made it feel safer. Sean and Loobey were all smiles as they spattered car bonnets and second-floor windows. Inside their fit and healthy bodies they felt invincible; nothing could catch them. They were teenagers having fun, but the last house they egged belonged to an ex-paratrooper without a sense of humour. The furious veteran bolted out of his house like a retired thorough-bred. While Sean, Loobey, Aaron, and Ryan had made a run for it, it soon became clear that Aaron, with his small legs, and Loobey, with his large belly, weren't going to make it. Ryan stopped dead in the middle of the road, a strap of terror tightening around his chest. His knees trembled, but he stood his ground while his friends and brother got away.

The paratrooper didn't slow down. He sprinted right through Ryan, knocking him to the ground so fiercely that he wondered if he'd been hit by a man or a bus. He slid across the uneven tarmac, arms and lower back shredding to pieces. The pain was immense, but the shock of being hit so suddenly and so hard was even worse.

Ryan remembered trying to get up, but the ex-paratrooper had kicked him in the head. Then, at some point while he was unconscious, Ryan's arm had been bent backwards and snapped at the elbow. It took six months to fully heal.

Ryan's mum had been furious, distraught, and had wasted no time in calling the police. The man who had attacked her boy was Neil Mitchell, and he had received eighteen months in HMP Wakefield and a nasty newspaper article written about him in the *Manchester Evening News*. Aaron had gone to his bedroom and had stayed there for the next nine years, surviving on Pot Noodles and video games. Ryan's stupid antics had traumatised his younger brother, who was already reeling from the loss of an uninterested father.

I'll never forgive myself for what he saw that day.

I just want him to grow up and be happy. That's the only way I'll know the damage I caused is healed.

"You okay, little brother?"

Aaron pulled his stick out of the stream and looked at Ryan. "I'm just worried about Sean. I know he's caused a lot of trouble, but I want him to be okay."

"Me too."

"I don't think he meant to hurt Tom."

"Me neither."

"No, Ryan, I mean he wasn't in control. When he bit Tom, it was after he'd got that green stuff all over his hands. What if it was already messing with his brain?"

Ryan considered it. It was a comforting thought, that Sean might not be to blame for his actions, but it felt like wishful thinking. He shook his head. "I don't think there was enough time between. He only had the oil on his hands for a couple of hours at most, and he first had a pop at Tom before we even went outside."

"But if he breathed it in or something? We don't know, do we? None of us has any clue what that stuff is up there." He turned and pointed to the hill rising behind the cottage.

"We'll know soon enough. It won't be much longer before Tom comes back with help. Then Sean will get whatever help he needs and life will go back to normal."

"Until you get married."

Ryan shifted slightly on the bank so that he was facing his brother. "What d'you mean?"

Aaron shrugged and went back to poking the water with his stick. "You're already hardly ever at home as it is. Once you're married, you'll be at Sophie's all the time."

"Well, yeah, that's what being married is. That's cool, though, right? You're growing up, Aaron. You should get a girl of your own."

Aaron didn't seem to be listening. "It's always been you and me, Ryan. Now it'll just be me and mam. It's gonna suck."

Ryan sighed. This was a conversation long on the cards. "Aaron, you're fifteen. You should have friends of your own and a couple of shags under your belt. It's not healthy wanting to spend all your time with me, or alone in your room."

"We're brothers, we stick together."

"Always, but that don't mean we can't have separate lives. When I'm gone, you need to step up and be a man. No more sitting around playing video games and wanking, okay? Toughen up, or this world will eat you alive, our kid."

Aaron tossed his stick into the stream and got up. He walked away without a word, so Ryan called out to him. When he didn't respond, he got up and went after him. "Aaron, stop! Talk to me. Where're you going?"

"I'm climbing the hill to take another look at that corkscrew. You wanted me to be a man, right?"

"That don't mean being stupid. You ain't going anywhere near that thing. It's dangerous."

"We were near it last night and we're fine. Sean's the only one with the fungus on him because he's the only one who touched it. I want to look at it in the light."

"Why? How will it help anything?"

"Maybe it won't, but either way, I'm going to climb the hill and take another look. If I don't, I'll just keep worrying about it."

Ryan cursed beneath his breath. What was this, a dick measuring contest? Aaron wanted to prove how fucking brave and stupid he was?

Yeah, that's exactly what this is. He's scared, and he's trying not to be. He's showing me he's stronger than I give him credit for.

"Okay, Aaron, if you're going back up that hill, then so am I."

"I can do it on my own. I don't need your help."

"I didn't say that you did, but you ain't going up there without me."

Aaron rolled his eyes. "Fine, just don't expect me to wait."

———

Climbing the hill was easier than it had been in the dark, and it took all of three minutes to go from the bottom to the top. In the muted morning sunlight, the summit seemed higher than it had beneath last night's moon.

And the corkscrew seemed much larger.

A part of Ryan had expected the strange artefact to be gone, so when he set his eyes on it, it took a moment for it to feel real. It was such an odd thing to be sitting on top of a grassy hill in the middle of nowhere. In the sunlight, the metallic surface was dark green, and the yellowish spots were amber. What none of them had noticed last night, however, was that the ground around the corkscrew was the same dark green colour as the oil on Sean's hands. While it could almost be mistaken for grass, it was too dark, and several rocky patches were also green where they should have been grey. The strange oil had soaked the ground.

"It must be some kind of chemical," said Aaron, stepping back so that his trainers were nowhere near the tainted soil. "It's leaking out of the corkscrew. Look!"

Green oil oozed from a series of holes at the bottom of the corkscrew. It sent a shiver down Ryan's spine as he zipped up his jacket and wrapped his arms around himself.

In matters such as these – matters of the strange – Aaron was more the expert than Ryan. His video games and Netflix education was infinitely superior. So Ryan deferred to his younger brother. "What could it be? Do you think it fell off a plane like Tom said?"

Aaron shrugged. "I think it's supposed to be buried in the ground like this. That's what a corkscrew does, right? It embeds itself. From the size of this section above ground, I reckon it must go down really deep. Ten feet, maybe more."

"What would be the point though? Why bury a corkscrew in the ground filled with some strange chemical?"

Aaron furrowed his brow in thought. The shy, socially stunted teenager gave way to an excited, confident young man, the mystery clearly something he enjoyed. "It could be a terraformer," was his first suggestion. "Maybe the government is working on a chemical to make unsuitable land better for farming. The green fuzz all over Sean, maybe it's like some kind of nutrient meant to enrich the soil." He looked down at their feet, at the spoiled grass and rocks. "It's spreading through the ground. Maybe it'll make all this rocky ground farmable."

Ryan chewed his top lip while he thought about it. If what Aaron said was true, it made a lot of sense. A third of the world was starving, hadn't he read that somewhere? If there was a chemical to make mountains and deserts farmable, it would be a massive triumph for mankind. "I want to believe you, little brother, but it all seems a little too easy to explain. Whatever this oil is, it's clearly dangerous – just look at Sean. The government wouldn't release something that wasn't safe, would they?"

Aaron shook his head incredulously. "Don't you know anything about the government?"

"They're not the villains from the movies, Aaron. The worst thing about the government is that they're incompetent and greedy."

Aaron smirked, clearly ready to continue the argument, but before he opened his mouth, he flinched and hopped back. "Whoa, what the hell!"

Ryan hopped away too. Insects covered a patch of earth near where Aaron had been standing. They were thick and slimy like slugs – except they had legs.

Ryan shuddered. "Are they some kind of beetle?"

"No." Aaron spoke confidently as he leaned over to examine the lumpy creatures about the size of an unshelled peanut. "They only have four legs. That doesn't make sense at all. Insects have six legs. Arachnids have eight. Only mammals have four, but no mammal is this small."

"You positive about that?"

Aaron shrugged. "I guess not."

Ryan watched as the tiny lumbering creatures stomped about on their four thick legs, and he could find no memory of ever seeing anything resembling them before. Not at the zoo. Not in an Attenborough special. "What are you saying?"

"That we need to capture one of them to show to Brett. Maybe it's a new species."

"No way. We're not touching those things."

Aaron wasn't listening. He was clearly fascinated. "They look like slugs, but they have thick little legs."

"Hey, we need to get down off this hill, okay? If it is something new, then they need to send a bunch of scientists up here to run tests and that. I'm sure we'll get the credit for finding it. We can name them Aaron Bugs. As in, Aaron bugs me because he won't listen to me."

Aaron started looking around, searching. "Hey, there's a water bottle over there."

Ryan nodded. "Loobey dropped it last night when Sean tried to grab him. So what?"

Aaron picked up the bottle and crouched beside the critters. "They're slow. I can catch one."

Ryan's skin was crawling by now, and the longer they stood there, the more insects – or not-insects – emerged from the earth. They seemed to be coming out of the ground around the base of the corkscrew. Had the massive chunk of metal unearthed some colony of undiscovered wildlife deep underground, or had they come out of the corkscrew itself? "Just hurry up and do what you need to do, okay? I'm freaking out here."

Aaron reached out towards one of the tiny bugs without hesitation, scooping the neck of the plastic water bottle into the green-tinged dirt and easily capturing the creature. It tumbled into the bottom of the container and immediately tried climbing up the sides. Whatever it was, it was cumbersome, and its attempts to escape proved futile.

Aaron held the bottle up to Ryan, beaming proudly. "See! Piece of piss."

"All right, smart arse. Can we go back down now?"

"You want me to hold your purse?"

Ryan rolled his eyes. "I'll be fine."

Aaron flinched. "Whoa!"

Ryan jolted. "Jeez, will you stop doing that!"

"The insect just squirted something." Aaron held up the bottle. Inside, the frantic creature had elongated, less a fat slug now and more of a slender beetle. Behind it, a green smear covered the plastic.

"It's the oil," said Ryan, stepping away. "Aaron, put it down."

"It's okay, it can't get out. Let's just get it to Brett."

"I don't like this."

"Hey, you said be a man. Maybe you should take your own advice. Panicking won't help anything, right? Let's just do this."

Ryan grunted. "Fine, but it's on your head if that thing escapes."

"It's just an insect, Ryan."

"No, little brother, you said it yourself. It's something else."

———

Brett and Loobey were looking under the Stelvio's hood when Ryan and Aaron returned. Brett was still clearly unnerved by the situation, but Loobey seemed focused on what he was doing. His forehead was sweaty and his expression grim as he prodded at the lifeless engine.

"See anything?" asked Brett, holding his glasses and chewing on one of the arms.

"Nah, it's the same as last night, mate. I hoped I'd see something in the daylight, but it all looks fine – not that I would really know."

"Still dead?" asked Ryan, the answer obvious.

Loobey dropped the bonnet down and wiped his hands on his tracksuit bottoms. "Dead as a donkey. To be honest, I only had a mooch because I was bored."

Brett surprised Ryan by grabbing an open beer from the roof of the car. He took a swig and glared. "Don't judge me, I'm on edge. Where the hell is Tom? It's been almost two hours."

"I'm sure he'll be along soon," said Ryan. "Anyway, we have something for you to look at. Show him, Aaron."

Aaron approached Brett cautiously, the plastic bottle held up before him like some kind of offering. "Check this out."

Brett squinted and leaned forward. "What is that?"

"We were hoping you could tell us," said Ryan. "We found it up on the hill, coming out of the ground next to the corkscrew."

"It only has four legs," said Aaron, clearly savouring the reveal.

"Impossible. All insects have six legs. It must have lost a couple when you picked it up."

Aaron shook his head. "There are a ton of them up there, and they all have four legs. They look just like this one."

"He's telling the truth," said Ryan. "Four legs, every one."

Brett moved his face right up to the bottle, but he didn't reach out to take it. "I've never seen anything like it. Some kind of slug, maybe, but with appendages. How did the green oil get inside the bottle?"

"The insect squirted it," said Aaron. "It's the same stuff Sean got on his hands, right?"

"I couldn't say. Possibly."

"We should kill it," said Loobey. "What if it's dangerous?"

Brett shrugged. "It may well be, but having a live specimen will help Sean if it ends up being related to the substance all over him. If it's some kind of toxin, this creature might help provide an antidote. Good job, Aaron."

Aaron beamed, but Ryan saw nothing to be happy about. Brett was a vet, but he had no clue about what was inside the bottle. How could that be anything but bad? Suddenly, the thought of discovering a new species was unappealing. He imagined the first person to discover a lion hadn't walked away to talk about it.

There was a noise from the cottage and everyone turned around. The front door had opened and Sean appeared on the front step. "Lads? What everyone doing out here?"

Brett moved away, holding his beer like he might use it as a weapon. Loobey moved away too, but Ryan was rooted to the spot. The sight of his friend was heartbreaking. More of the strange green fuzz had turned black and crusty, and Sean's entire stomach now looked like it had been singed by flame, except for the bony protuberance he had uncovered earlier on his stomach. His left eye was completely ravaged, the fuzz now creeping down towards the edges of his mouth. His ribs showed through his flesh. Had Sean been so skinny when he had arrived at the cottage? Was the fungus eating him alive? Using him as fuel?

Killing him?

Suddenly, Ryan realised there was a strong chance that Sean was going to die. Whatever was happening to him was clearly catastrophic. "Y-You should go back inside, Sean. You need to rest."

Sean's lower lip quivered. "Please, Ryan, don't make me stay inside when you're all out here. I'm so hot. I feel like I'm on fire. Please, can I just stay out here with you? I don't want to be on my own."

Ryan glanced at Loobey and Brett. Brett was shaking his head. Loobey had tears in his eyes. Sean looked so afraid, so weak and alone.

"I-I'm going down to the stream," said Aaron, forcing a smile to his face to remove the revulsion. "D'you want to come with me, Sean?"

Ryan looked at his younger brother. "Aaron, what are you doing?"

"He's our friend. If you all want to keep your distance, fine, but I'm going to look after him."

Sean was smiling, a massive relief clearly washing over him. He was so frail, like a little old man being asked to go out on a walk. "Y-Yes, I want to see the stream. I want to see the water."

"Come on then, it's just down here. Keep back a little though, okay? You're not very well and I don't want to catch it."

Sean nodded even more enthusiastically. "No problem, our kid. I'll keep my hands to meself, I swear down."

Sean hobbled towards Aaron, not noticing that Brett and Loobey were cowering away from him. Aaron smiled warmly and told him that everything would be okay.

Ryan felt a pain in his chest and a stinging in his eyes. These could be Sean's final moments, and his friends were abandoning him. "Wait, I'll join you."

Aaron shrugged like it was no big deal. "You want to grab a few beers then? I think Sean could use one."

Sean started laughing, a weak and brittle sound. "I don't half."

Ryan went inside the cottage to fetch some beers. His hands were shaking as he opened the fridge, and the hairs on the back of his neck stood up as he felt a presence behind him. He straightened up to see Brett and Loobey standing behind him in the kitchenette.

"You need to keep Aaron away from him," said Brett. "His infection is worse than it was a couple of hours ago. It's spreading fast. It's all over him."

"You don't think I know that. I'll make sure Aaron is safe. That's why I'm going."

"None of us are safe with Sean walking around. He's a goddamn biological hazard."

Loobey winced. "He's just ill. It's not his fault."

"So what? It's not worth risking our lives for, is it? He's contagious and we need to stay away. It's not like he has cancer."

Ryan couldn't help it, his eyes went to Loobey. His friend gave him a pleading expression. *Don't do it,* was the message. Brett caught the silent exchange and grew suspicious. "What? What is it?"

Loobey shook his head at Ryan, but Ryan couldn't keep a secret. It had hurt, finding out that Loobey had kept the cancer secret from him, and he couldn't do the same thing to Brett. "Loobey has cancer."

Loobey groaned. "Fuck, man, you promised."

"We're your mates, Loobey. We can help you."

"Are you an oncologist, Ryan? Because if you're not, then you can't help me at all."

"You know what I mean."

"No. I don't."

"Wait," said Brett. "Loobey, you have cancer? What's the prognosis?"

Loobey sighed and leaned against the counter. The sweat on his forehead came in beads. "It's no picnic, but I'm dealing with it. It is what it is."

"I'm sorry," said Brett. "My nan had breast cancer in her fifties. She survived, but I know she went through hell. What kind do you have?"

"Hodgkin's lymphoma. It's cancer of the lymphatic system. I don't know the ins and outs of it – I kind of block my ears when the doctors get too technical – but it's treatable and I'm being treated. End of."

Brett took in a deep breath and steadied himself. "Okay. We don't have to talk about it, Loobs, but if you need anything, I'm here."

"Thanks. I just want to get on with things."

"Of course, but if you have cancer, then it's even more important that you stay away from Sean. With your compromised immune system, you're in greater danger than any of us."

Loobey grabbed a beer from the fridge and took a swig. "This is probably going to make me puke, but I need it."

Brett put a hand on the counter and shoved aside some of the snacks until he found something he seemed to be searching for. It was a packet of salted peanuts. "Here, eat these while you drink. I read once that they can help with nausea."

"Really?"

"It's probably an old wives' tale, but you never know. Eat a couple after every sip. See how you go."

Loobey took a swig of beer and gasped with pleasure, then munched on a handful of peanuts. He seemed to loosen up. "Oh, sweet intoxicating poison. Just what the doctor ordered."

Brett turned to Ryan. "You need to keep Sean away from the cottage until Tom gets back. If you and Aaron want to risk your health, that's your choice, but keep him away from Loobey and me."

"Fine. Let's just hope no one else gets infected, if this is the way we behave."

"I'm just being practical, Ryan. Keep yourself and Aaron as far away from Sean as possible, okay? And at all costs, do not let him touch you."

"I get it, but I can't abandon him. You saw how pathetic he was. How afraid he was."

"He's dying," said Loobey. When they looked at him, he sighed and went on. "I've spent enough time around cancer wards to know the look. If Tom doesn't get back soon, Sean ain't gonna make it."

Brett cleared his throat, ran a hand across his forehead. "I don't know what we're dealing with, but based on his rapidly increasing emaciation, I would have to agree. The fungus is draining his reserves. Get him to eat something, Ryan, if you can."

Ryan grabbed a packet of crisps to accompany the beers. "I'll do my best. What are you two going to do while I'm back at the stream?"

"Wait for Tom," said Brett. "What else *is* there to do?"

"Drink," said Loobey, holding up his beer, "to our health."

CHAPTER SEVEN

R yan joined Aaron and Sean by the stream. There was a good
three metres between the two of them and Sean appeared
calm with his bare feet in the water. The fact that he was naked bar
a pair of boxer shorts didn't seem to concern him. Ryan was
wearing his jacket and still felt a crisp chill.

"You okay, Sean?" asked Ryan.

Sean twisted around, a weak smile on his green and pale face.
"Just enjoying the scenery, mate. Not every day you get to enjoy
fresh air like this. It can add years to your life."

Ryan plonked himself down on Sean's left, Aaron already sitting
on his right. He stared down the hillside as his lungs took in the
clean air, absorbing the grey-green-orange landscape that seemed
to stretch on forever. "This is why I picked the place. I wanted to
make some memories."

"Job done," Aaron muttered. Once again he was poking at the
water with a stick. "None of us is ever going to forget this."

Ryan had to concede his brother's point, although he could
have done without the tone. "Things didn't exactly go the way I
expected, but we're going to get through this. How're you feeling,
Sean?"

Sean shrugged, as if to suggest he was fine, but a small amount
of that calm gave way to panic. The sudden pleading look in his
one good eye made it seem like he was a prisoner trapped inside his

own body. When he spoke, it seemed to take great effort. "W-What's happening to me, Ryan?"

"You're going to be just fine, Sean."

"I don't believe you. I can see it in your face, man. This ain't gonna get better, is it?"

"Brett said it's just a fungus. Medicine will treat it. As soon as Tom gets back with help, we'll get you seen to. Right as rain, you'll be."

"It's too late, Ryan. There's all this noise inside my head. It's like screaming, hundreds of people screaming at me. I... I'm scared. I'm really scared."

Ryan wanted to reach out and hold his friend, but the green fuzz was all over his body, right up to his throat. It was like sitting next to a monster – something human in shape only. Ryan did the only thing he could think of. He rolled a beer across the bank and tossed the packet of crisps. "Here, try to eat something, okay?"

Sean reached out to take the beer but changed his mind and put his hand in his lap. His fuzzy fingers rested against the strange bone-like protrusion on his stomach. The desperate, frightened look in his eye had gone. "I'm not thirsty."

"Oh, okay. Do you mind if I drink? I know it's early, but my nerves are fried."

"Fine." That was all Sean said. He sat completely still, staring into the water.

Ryan tossed Aaron a beer behind Sean's back and opened one for himself. They both took a swig and exchanged nervous glances with one another. For a second, Sean had been himself – afraid and confused, but himself. Now he was a zombie, staring at nothing.

Aaron rattled something on the ground in front of him. It was the plastic bottle with the critter inside. Ryan groaned. "Are you still carrying that thing around?"

"Brett thinks we need to keep it, for the antidote or whatever."

"Sean isn't poisoned. Brett has no idea what he's talking about."

Aaron rattled the bottle, knocking the critter about inside. There was now green oil all over the bottom section. "Brett said I was right to capture it, so I'm holding onto it. Look, there's more of the green oil on the plastic and..."

"What?"

"The fungus. It's growing along the bottom. See?"

Ryan had to get up and go around Sean to take a closer look, and at first, he saw nothing. Then he noticed the narrow seam of fuzz growing along the bottom edge of the bottle. "It's the same as..." He glanced at Sean. "It's the same."

Sean flinched, making them both jump. "What you got there? What you got?"

"Um..." Aaron raised the plastic bottle and rattled it. "Just something we found on top of the hill."

Sean suddenly growled, his fuzz-encrusted left eye twitching. "Let it go."

Ryan frowned. "What are you talking about, Sean? It's just a bug we found."

Sean leapt up, landing on his feet like a cat. He bared his teeth, several of them covered by a slimy green mould. A stale odour escaped his mouth. Ryan panicked, wondering if the stench meant he was breathing something in. He took a step back, moving Aaron behind him.

Sean crouched, like he was preparing to pounce. "Let. It. Go."

"No," said Aaron. "This can help the doctors figure out what's wrong with you. We need to keep—"

Sean snatched at him.

Ryan pushed Aaron out of the way and then threw himself to the floor to avoid Sean's attack. He quickly rolled along the rocky embankment until he was back up on his feet. Sean followed him, preparing to leap again. He bent at the knees, scowling at Ryan like he wished him dead. The fuzz in his eye began to quiver, something festering within.

"Bugs!" said Aaron. "There are bugs coming out of his eye."

Ryan covered his mouth with a hand as Sean's left eye ruptured and a disgusting mass of foul brown liquid spilled down his cheek. The liquid was filled with tiny slug-like creatures, matching those they had found on the hill.

Ryan dodged backwards, horrified by what he saw. "Sean, stay the hell back!"

Sean was beyond words; he lunged at Ryan again. Ryan kicked out and planted a foot in his stomach, sending him backwards. The bony patch beneath Sean's belly button broke open and more brown slime oozed from his body. More four-legged slugs erupted from his flesh, raining down onto the grass with a *pitter-patter*.

Sean attacked again, a large flap of his stomach now hanging open and revealing his decaying insides. This time he didn't lunge; he came forward with his arms outstretched, hissing and snarling like a ghoul.

"Sean, stay back! The hell is wrong with you?"

"It's in his brain," said Aaron. "He isn't in control of himself."

Ryan backed away, hands out, pleading. Begging. "Sean, don't!"

"Our kid," said Sean, before lunging at Ryan's throat.

There was nothing in Ryan's hands except an opened can of beer. Instinctively, he chucked the contents in Sean's face, blinding his one functioning eye and disorientating him long enough to get out of the way.

Aaron grabbed Ryan's arm and pulled him backwards. "We need to leg it."

"No shit! Come on!"

Sean tried to block their retreat, but Aaron tossed the plastic bottle with the bug inside. It sailed past Sean and landed in the stream, causing him to turn around to retrieve it. Was he concerned about the bug's welfare?

Ryan and Sean raced up the hill. The cottage wasn't far, but Ryan wished he had wings so he could fly there. His hopes for Sean disintegrated as he became certain that his oldest friend was done for. Surely there was no cure for whatever was happening to him. There would be no treatment that would lead to them all laughing about this a month from now. There was no happy ending to whatever this was.

Brett and Loobey were on the driveway. Loobey was sitting on the front step. Brett was perched on the bonnet of Tom's car. They were drinking beer and chatting, and when they saw Ryan and Aaron sprinting for their lives, they seemed confused. What else could they be? How could they know that Sean was leaking bugs and trying to kill them?

"Get inside," yelled Ryan. "Get inside the cottage." Brett shook his head and mouthed something. Clearly, he didn't understand. "Sean has lost it. Get inside the house!"

Brett still didn't seem to get it, but Loobey stood up from the step. It wasn't enough of a reaction, and Ryan was frustrated when he finally reached the driveway. He clutched his side, struggling with a stitch, but he bellowed at his friends full force. "We need to go inside right now. Sean is out of his mind."

Loobey shoved the door open. "All right, man, I'm going!"

Aaron and Loobey hurried inside, but Brett remained standing near the car, looking towards the stream. "I don't see Sean coming. What happened?"

"I'll explain inside. Please, just trust me. The shit has hit the fan." Unbelievably, Brett still didn't make a move towards the cottage. He continued looking around, searching for Sean. Ryan grabbed him. "I know you're the smart one, Brett, but right now you need to accept what I'm telling you and get inside the cottage. Right fucking now!"

"Okay, okay, calm down."

"I'll calm down inside."

They both turned towards the front door, just in time to see something bolt inside before them. When they heard Loobey cry out, they panicked and got going. Brett entered the lounge first and immediately skidded to a halt. Ryan did the exact same thing a second later.

What the hell is happening? This can't be real.

Aaron was kicking wildly and trying to defend himself. Loobey grabbed a can of beer from the counter and tossed it across the room. It struck a large rabbit on the flanks and caused it to spin around in the centre of the lounge. Its dark eyes were crusted around the edges. Its light brown coat was stained green in places. Bugs festered in its fur, a sea of movement.

The rabbit leapt at Loobey, but Loobey hopped up on the counter and yanked his legs out of the way. Aaron took a run up and booted the rabbit in the undercarriage, sending it airborne. The sound of the animal's ribs breaking echoed off the low ceiling as it bounced off the arm of the sofa and landed on its back. It immediately corrected itself, resuming its attack. Its long incisors were mottled, white and green, and a patch of dark fuzz was peeling away from its hind leg. Beneath was the same bony material that covered Sean's stomach.

Ryan willed his legs to move, mortally afraid for himself, his brother, and his friends. He made it halfway across the lounge before he caught the rabbit's attention, but the sight of it racing towards him rooted him to the spot. This small animal should have been no threat, but instead it was a thrashing ball of teeth and claws. Ryan turned himself, intending to launch the hardest kick he could muster. If he was lucky, he would crush the rabbit's skull and kill it. If he was *unlucky*...

The rabbit leapt into the air with a furious squeal, powerful hind legs propelling it right at Ryan's throat. Any chance of kicking it went right out of the window, as he could do nothing but shield himself now.

I'm gonna die on my stag do, gored to death by sodding Peter Rabbit.

Brett shoved Ryan aside and caught the airborne rabbit in his jacket. He quickly dumped it to the floor before pinning it against the floorboards. Underneath the jacket, the crazed rabbit thrashed and squealed.

"Help me," said Brett, not fearfully, but testily. "Hurry up."

Aaron and Ryan looked at each other, neither knowing what to do. Loobey hopped down off the counter and lifted up a full box of beer. He clutched it against his waist and toddled over to the rabbit trapped beneath the jacket. "Calm down and have a drink," he said, and then dropped the box of beer on top of the coat.

The rabbit was clearly stunned, its movements no longer frantic, but jerky and slow. Loobey bent down, picked the beer back up, and threw it down a second time with added force.

The rabbit went still.

Loobey collapsed on the sofa, panting, while everyone else stared at the misshapen lump beneath Brett's jacket.

Suddenly, Aaron shouted, "Ryan, the door!"

Ryan turned, expecting to see Sean. Instead, he saw a fox, its red and white fur spoiled by the green oil. It stared in at them hungrily.

Ryan wasted no time. He raced across the lounge and slammed the door closed just as the fox made a move to enter the cottage. It scratched against the wood, letting out a strange mewing sound. Ryan dropped the latch and leaned against the door, taking deep breaths and trying not to faint. He felt sick. Dizzy. Exhausted.

Terrified.

Aaron yelled again. "Shit! Bugs!"

Not knowing how much more he could take, Ryan looked over to see his brother stamping on the floorboards. From beneath Brett's jacket, an army of the slug-like creatures had emerged. Brett raced to help, jumping up and down on the bugs like an excited toddler. Despite their thick legs, the creatures were slow-moving, and within a minute a squashed mess stained the floorboards.

Ryan turned to face the front door, sweat soaking his hair. He peered out of the small diamond-shaped window and thought about only one thing.

Where's Sean?

———

"This is insane," said Brett. His philosophy of not touching had gone out of the window as he attempted to make Loobey comfortable on the couch. Picking up – and slamming – the box of beer had clearly taken it out of Loobey, and he was now as pale as a freshly laundered bed sheet. With Brett's swollen ankle and Tom's severed ear, only Ryan and Aaron remained in full health.

"This is insane," Brett said again.

Ryan gripped the kitchen counter, still dizzy from the battle with the rabbit. "As long as we stay inside, we'll be fine."

We'll be fine.

After closing the front door, Aaron and Ryan had pushed the armchair up against it. Then they had drawn the curtains over the windows, turned off the lights, and kept their voices down. The fox outside had seemingly gone away. Nothing was trying to get inside. It felt safe, but Ryan knew it was an illusion.

We're not safe in here. We're trapped in here.

Aaron was sitting on the smaller of the two sofas, staring at the lumpy mound beneath Brett's jacket. "The animals are infected with the same thing Sean has." He was seemingly talking to himself. "It's the bugs. The bugs were all over the rabbit. The bugs produce the oil and it turns into the fungus."

"That doesn't make any sense," said Brett. "Creatures can produce venom or toxins, but they can't produce life forms separate from themselves. The only thing I can assume is that the insects are themselves infected with some kind of organism that takes control of them and uses them as a means to spread. It's not unheard of in nature."

"It's taken control of Sean, too," said Aaron. "He's violent and confused."

"Wasn't he always?"

"You know what I mean."

Brett folded his arms and leaned back against the kitchen counter beside Ryan. "Increased violence has been shown in sufferers of the rabies virus, so I suppose it's possible that Sean's behaviour could be a result of infection. Of course, this isn't rabies we're talking about, not by a long shot. This is like nothing I've ever read about or studied, or even heard of. It's like something from a horror film."

"Yeah, *Attack of the Fuzzy Green Zombies*," said Loobey, lying on his back and taking deep breaths.

"Sean's not a zombie," said Aaron. "It was more like he was angry and confused."

Brett went into the lounge and handed Loobey a bottle of water, then placed his hand against his sweaty forehead. "You're burning up, Loobs." He looked at his watch. "Where the hell is Tom? He should have come back by now. What is it to the village? Two miles?"

Ryan shrugged. "More or less. The road isn't easy, though. He's probably had to take it slow."

Brett nodded but didn't seem to believe it. Out of all of them, he was the most on edge. Just looking at him made Ryan feel guilty for putting him in this situation.

Aaron slid off the sofa and knelt beside Brett's jacket. Everyone tensed, Ryan most of all. "Aaron, what are you doing?"

"I want to look at the rabbit. Maybe we can learn something."

"What the hell are we going to learn by looking at a dead rabbit?"

"Brett should take a look. He's a vet."

Brett grimaced, but slowly his expression changed. "I'm not an expert in contagious organisms, but I suppose it might help if we can find out how the infection progresses."

"How it *progresses*?" Ryan was unsettled by the word.

"Don't you want to know which organs it affects? How it spreads?"

"No, not really."

"I do," said Aaron. "I want to know what we're up against." Without asking for permission, he whipped away Brett's jacket, revealing a pile of rotting brown flesh and clumps of green fuzz. The rabbit's glassy eyes stared at the front door, as if it might get up and try to escape.

Ryan covered his nose with his forearm. "It fucking reeks."

Aaron moved away in revulsion, too. Brett, however, probably used to blood and guts, leaned right over the corpse. "It's completely desiccated." There was wonderment in his voice. "The fungus fed on the rabbit's organs, probably using it as fuel to spread outside the body."

"There's more of that bony stuff," said Aaron, pointing at the rabbit's guts while pulling the neck of his T-shirt up over his mouth and nose.

Ryan grimaced, not understanding how his brother could be so curious about something so gross. All the same, he wanted to add to the conversation. "With Sean, the bone cracked open and bugs spilled out."

"Get me a pen," said Brett.

The small console table next to the front door had a guest's comments book. On top of the book was a red biro. Ryan grabbed it and handed it to Brett, being sure to keep his distance from the squashed rabbit.

Brett used the biro to poke at the corpse, specifically at the bony protuberance. "It's not bone," he said. "It's fibrous, more like chitin."

"What the hell is chitin?" Loobey had rolled onto his side and was watching them intently.

"It's the substance you usually find in insects and sea creatures. Insects have their skeletons on the outside, right? Think of a scorpion or a beetle. They don't have skeletons like us, they have shells. Chitin is the stuff those shells are typically made of. It can be very thick, like with a crab, but also thin enough to form the wings of a dragonfly. It's one of the most common biological components on

Earth. In this case, it seems to have formed some kind of protective sac."

"For the insects," said Aaron.

Brett adjusted his glasses, took a moment, and then sighed. "It seems like the insects are the vectors for the fungus. They're born inside an infected creature. Once they're mature enough, they escape their protective sac and start spreading the green oil. The green oil leads to more fungus that in turn leads to more infected animals, which leads to more insects. It's a complete life cycle. The only problem is that this organism is entirely unknown to science."

"How can you be sure?" asked Ryan, holding his nose to combat the smell. It made him sound bunged up, like he had a cold. "You don't know every species of animal."

Brett gave a slightly defensive smile. "Of course I don't, but vets don't study thirty thousand separate species of spider to know about spiders. They study a few of the most common species along with a small collection of outliers. By doing this they can make an educated guess about all of the species in between. Same goes for all other animal species. Learn the biology of a Havana rabbit and you can be pretty confident about the biology of a Florida White."

"What's your point?"

"His point," said Aaron, "is that he might not know every fungus or insect, but he knows enough to realise when something isn't right."

Brett nodded. "Exactly. I understand enough to be sure that what we're dealing with isn't in any textbook, the bugs and the fungus, both."

For some reason, Ryan was irritated. He wanted answers, but all he was getting were reasons to be afraid. "So what are you saying? Did some new species emerge from the earth right next to this cottage in the middle of nowhere, disturbed by that chunk of metal falling out of the sky because a plane forgot to lock its cargo hatch?"

"These hills and mountains are ancient, and mostly untouched. For all we know, this organism could be prehistoric, lying inert beneath the soil for thousands of years until a big chunk of porous metal came and provided a route to the surface."

"What if the metal didn't come from a plane?" said Aaron. "What if it came from higher up? Like, from aliens?"

Everyone tutted.

Aaron blushed, but he was defiant. "You don't know! What if the corkscrew was launched from space by an alien civilisation?"

Ryan rolled his eyes. "To do what?"

"To take over. What if the bugs are alien life forms, and the fungus is a way of infecting Earth – or altering it? Maybe it's an alien plot to make the planet suitable for them to come here and take it for themselves."

"I don't like how convincing he's making this sound," said Loobey. "He's talking bollocks, right? Brett?"

"Once again," said Brett, visibly annoyed. "I'm just a vet. You're asking me whether or not we're being invaded by aliens? Seriously?"

"Is it possible?" asked Ryan, ignoring his protests.

Brett sighed. "Isn't *anything* possible? It's far more likely that something was in stasis beneath the soil, but, yes, sure, why not, let's assume it's aliens. They have to exist somewhere, right? Maybe Aaron is right, and this is a biological attack in order to terraform the planet." He had sounded serious for a moment, but slowly the sarcasm crept into his voice. "Two weeks from now, our planet will be covered in green fungus and Oscar the Grouch will become our new overlord. Look, guys, whatever this is, it's a hundred per cent terrestrial. The fungus is thriving in our atmosphere, which means it must have come from here. An alien life form would likely need a set of conditions so completely different from ours that it would be incomprehensible. Organisms grow and adapt to suit their environment, not the other way around. They evolve in sync with the unique biomes they are born into. The chances of our Earth being in any way compatible for an alien lifeform is extremely unlikely." He sighed and rubbed at his temples. "Christ, you've got me talking about aliens like it's a real possibility. This is *not* aliens. It's dangerous as hell, but we are going to sit tight and wait for help, okay? Once it arrives, someone else can figure it all out. What I can tell you is that if we catch it, we're screwed. This rabbit has no insides. For all intents and purposes, it was dead when it attacked us. The fungus has ravaged its central nervous system and reduced its biological imperatives to just one thing – attack."

Aaron licked his lips, finally showing fear instead of awe. "Because attacking means spreading the fungus, right?"

Brett exhaled. "Sean wasn't trying to hurt you, he was trying to infect you. We need to make sure nothing gets in here. No more rabbits, no foxes, and most definitely not Sean."

Ryan looked over at the windows, realising that curtains weren't going to be enough.

———

"Help me get this up against the window." Ryan grunted and fought with the fridge, which he had dragged out of the kitchenette. He could wave goodbye to his deposit after the mess he'd made of the floorboards. Twin gouges ran all the way across the lounge like a set of railroad tracks. The fridge was currently snagged on a wire leading to the lamp on the console table.

Aaron moved the lamp and its wire out of the way, then helped his brother slide the fridge up against one of the two windows in the lounge. Fortunately, the cottage wasn't large, which meant there was a decent chance of barricading themselves inside with the meagre resources they had. The master bedroom's window was now blocked by a heavy oak wardrobe, and the small window in the kitchen was locked tight and secured. Upstairs was less of a concern, but they had double-checked all of the windows anyway.

Morning had passed and it was now afternoon. Bright sunshine crept in through the slender gaps between the curtains and through the window diamond set into the top of the front door. The diamond was their portal to the outside, and Ryan stared out of it regularly. Nothing seemed to be on the driveway, but somehow that made things worse. Where the hell was Sean? What was he doing?

"Tom should definitely be back by now," said Brett, lining up kitchen knives on the counter. Only a couple of them were long enough to do any real damage.

"Something happened to him," said Aaron, sitting on the big blue sofa. "What other explanation is there?"

Loobey was on the smaller beige sofa, sipping from a bottle of water. He had managed to catch his breath, and a smidge of colour had returned to his cheeks. "There *isn't* another explanation," he said. "Who knows how many infected animals are out there? He could've been attacked by anything."

Aaron turned away from the fridge, now in place by the window. "Like what?"

Brett left his knives and folded his arms. "Stags can be territorial. Highland cows can trample you to death if you rub one up the wrong way. Even a fox can give you a nasty bite – especially if their inhibitions are impeded by a rapidly growing fungus. Hell, a rat can kill a human being if it's determined enough. Graveyards are full of dead idiots who thought it was a good idea to pet something fluffy. We're in the wilderness. It belongs to the animals, not us."

Aaron's head dropped. "What if Tom's just hurt? He could be out there somewhere, praying for help."

Nobody argued. Nobody spoke.

The cottage was barricaded as well as it could be, which left them with nothing to do but sit and wait for something to happen. With any luck, that *something* would be help arriving. Tom was a grown man. They had to trust that he could reach the village one way or another.

Brett took a seat on the large sofa and began tapping at his phone. "I still don't understand what's happened to this thing," he said. "I've had it on charge for the last thirty minutes and it's still not switching on."

"Hold on a sec," said Aaron, and he disappeared into the back bedroom. He reappeared a moment later, holding an iPad. "I charged this before Ryan and I set off." He held the power button on the top and waited. And waited. After another moment, he tutted and placed the tablet down on the kitchen counter. "It won't switch on either. Loobey, try the TV."

Loobey leaned forward and grabbed the remote, which had miraculously stayed on the coffee table since their arrival. He pointed it at the small flat screen in the corner and pressed a button. A nearly undetectable flash of light, but then nothing. Loobey grunted. "Nowt's happening."

Ryan frowned. Outside, the generator continued to hum. He looked over at the lamp on the console table. It was switched on and glowing brightly. He went into the kitchen to try the appliances. The microwave was dead, but the hob burners came on when he pressed the electric igniter button. The kettle boiled without issue. "I don't get it. Some things turn on and others don't."

"EMP," said Aaron. He almost shouted it, and his face lit up like he had the answer for everything. "The lights and the kettle switch on because they don't have computers in them. A light is just a simple circuit. So is the element in a kettle, I suppose." He tapped a finger against his chin, clearly trying to figure things out. "Our phones and tablets have computers. The TV looks modern, so it's probably a smart TV."

"Tom's car is smart too," said Loobey. "It's filled with gadgets and screens. Almost drove *itself* here. The satnav, the keyless ignition... It's all computers, man. I read something about new cars having more lines of code in them than the computers NASA used to put people on the moon."

Ryan looked at his brother. "So what are you saying? EMP is like a shockwave, right? A blast that knocks out all of the electronics?"

Aaron grew animated, excited once more as things re-entered his geeky wheelhouse of Internet conspiracy theories and cheesy special-effects laden movies. "The military are working on all kinds of EMP devices to knock out enemy infrastructure. When that corkscrew landed on the hill, it must have sent out a massive pulse."

"The earthquake," said Loobey. "We all felt it."

"Hold on," said Brett. "First, you were telling us that the corkscrew is some kind of alien canister meant to transform Earth. Now you're saying it's a military EMP device? EMP can be caused by many things, even lightning, but modern computers and equipment are shielded from the effects."

Aaron narrowed his eyes. "How do you even know about EMP? You're a vet."

"I'm a vet that likes to read science fiction in his spare time. There are dozens of books about EMP scenarios, which is why I know it would take something monumental to take out our phones – a nuclear blast or an unprecedented solar storm, that kind of thing."

Aaron's eyes went wide. "How about an alien artefact crashing through our atmosphere? Would that do it? It's that thing on the hill, I'm telling you. It could all be part of what I said earlier about aliens readying the planet for invasion. Knocking out communications sounds like a good way to help an infection spread, don't you think? We can't call for help. We can't warn anyone."

Brett tossed his useless phone down on the counter, rattling the knives he had placed there. "We are not being invaded by aliens. I'm more inclined to believe your imbecilic theories about military weapons. Grow the hell up, Aaron."

Aaron flinched. "Sorry, I was just—"

"Just keep your stupid fantasies to yourself, okay? It's just worrying everyone."

Ryan glared at Brett across the counter. "He's just a kid, man, and he's as freaked out as the rest of us."

"Exactly," said Brett, "he's just a kid. What the hell were you thinking bringing him along on a stag do?"

"I assumed I could trust my mates to show him a good time and keep him safe."

Brett huffed and folded his arms. "And how's that going?"

"Back off, Brett. Having a pop isn't going to help, is it? We all came here because we're mates."

"Are we? I mean, *really*, are we mates? I haven't seen you in six months. I haven't seen Sean in even longer. I'm assuming you haven't seen much of Tom either? We've moved on with our lives, Ryan. We have careers and other interests. I don't understand your fixation on trying to keep us all together. What was so great about the old days that you miss them so much? Was it drinking ourselves stupid every night of the week? Or was it never having any money? Is your life really so awful that you want to stay stuck in the past? Newsflash, Ryan, but the past was awful."

Ryan reeled, taking Brett's words like a blast to the face. "What are you talking about? We were inseparable. The laughs we used to have..."

"The laughs might have seemed worth it at the time, but I'm embarrassed about the things we used to get up to. It's a miracle none of us ended up in prison or a coffin. We were idiots, and I don't miss it at all. I finally have my life exactly how I want it, and unfortunately that doesn't include the likes of Sean or—" Brett shook his head and turned away.

Or you. That's what he was about to say.

Ryan's body betrayed him and a tear spilled down his cheek. He quickly wiped it away, trying to hold onto the anger instead of letting it give way to sadness. With all that was happening, it was getting harder and harder to keep himself together. "I always knew you would end up doing something great with your life, Brett. You were always so smart, so dedicated. There was no question that you would succeed. I just didn't realise the kind of person you would turn into."

Brett kept his back turned. "I'm not going to feel guilty for growing up. If you had any—"

"I was just disposable to you, huh?" Ryan shook his head, more disappointed than angry. "Just a mate to fill the time while you worked towards something better, yeah? Well, thanks for using me for the last ten years, mate. Feels great."

Brett turned around. He pulled off his glasses and glared. "I didn't *use* you. We grew apart, like most people do when they become adults and other things become priorities. You should be planning a future with Sophie, not looking back at the past and wishing you were still living it. You don't even *want* to get married, do you?"

Ryan glanced at Loobey, wondering if he had shared last night's conversation as revenge for Ryan spilling the beans about his cancer, but nothing about Loobey's expression suggested he had said anything to Brett.

When Ryan failed to answer, Brett gave a smug grin. "You see? You're terrified to grow up, but it's your issue, not mine. Stop blaming everybody else and accept the truth that you're just drifting through life without a purpose. How many jobs have you had since leaving school? A dozen?"

Loobey grimaced on the sofa. "Come on, Brett, that's enough."

Ryan felt his fists clench. His upper lip curled into a snarl. "D'you agree with him, Loobey? You've been ill for months and you never fucking told me. Am I deluding myself by thinking we're all mates? Am I an idiot?"

"Of course not. I love you, man, and I always will, but part of what Brett said is right. Eventually, the fun ends, you know? Adult responsibilities come along and suddenly there's less time to hang out. It's happened to us all, and so slowly we didn't even notice. I used to spend the weekends on the lash, but now I spend them with my daughter. Brett and Tom have demanding jobs. We don't have the free time we used to. It sucks, but it's life. As for why I didn't tell you about my cancer, well, I just didn't want you to have to drop everything to be there for me. I knew that if I told you, you would put your own life on hold, and that wouldn't be fair."

Ryan turned and headed for the door.

"Where are you going?" Aaron asked, following after him.

"I'm walking to the village. I can't stay here."

"Then I'm coming with you."

Ryan wanted to hug him, but he wouldn't do it in front of the others. Instead, he smiled at his brother and gave a nod. "Thanks."

Loobey got up of the sofa. "Ryan, just sit down, okay? It's not safe to go outside."

"Fuck you, Loobey."

"Seriously? You're gonna be like that?"

"You see," said Brett. "This is what I'm talking about. You're storming off like a child instead of facing the truth. It's pathetic and it's going to get you killed."

Ryan spun around and pointed a finger at Brett. It took a moment to get his words out because his jaw was locked so tightly in anger. "You listen to me, if you—"

There was a banging at the door. The wood rattled in its frame.

Everyone froze except for Ryan, who turned around slowly. "Um... Hello?"

"Ryan? It's me, Sean. You need to let me in. You need to let me in right now."

CHAPTER EIGHT

R yan slid the armchair aside slightly and tried to see Sean
through the window diamond in the door. The only thing he
could see, however, was his friend's shadow on the driveway.

"Do *not* let him in here," said Brett, and he grabbed the biggest
knife from the collection on the counter. "I swear to God, do not
open that door, Ryan."

Ryan put a finger against his lips to quieten Brett, then
returned his focus to the door. "Sean, can you move where I can
see you?"

"Why?"

"Because I need to know if you're okay. You're ill, Sean. You
tried to attack Aaron and me by the stream."

Silence, and then, "Sorry about that, our kid. I didn't want to
tell you, but I did some more blow this morning. Sent me a bit
doolally and that. I'm fine now though, I swear down. Let me in,
Ryan. It's freezing out here and I'm dying of thirst."

"I can't do that. You could be infectious."

"There's nowt wrong with me. Whatever was on me has dried
up and fell off. I'm right as rain, me."

Brett glanced at the others in the room. They seemed as
doubtful as Ryan was. "Then step in front of the door so that I can
see you."

"Give over, mate. My tits are turning blue out here."

Loobey sat forward on the sofa, his palms against his cheeks. "He's lying."

Ryan nodded. Of course Sean was lying. "You're not coming in here, mate. I'm sorry."

"What about some water then? Just open the door and hand me a bottle."

"I can't do that."

Silence for a moment, and then Sean's footsteps retreated on the gravel.

Ryan breathed a sigh of relief. "He's going."

"He sounded normal," said Aaron. "Like himself."

"Impossible," said Brett. "There's no way he's okay. We all saw him this morning. He was close to death."

Ryan peered through the window diamond, trying to see Sean on the driveway. He caught a slight movement to the right, assuming it was Sean walking away. But he wasn't walking away.

"Shit!" Ryan leapt back as Sean sprinted at the door and threw himself against the wood. The entire frame shook, and the window diamond shattered as a twisted arm punched through it. Sean's hand was skeletal, coated in a syrupy brown substance that was infested with insects. The tiny four-legged bugs dropped onto the floorboards and began to scuttle. Ryan yelled in terror and began stomping on them. Aaron and the others came to help.

"Let me in," Sean snarled from behind the door. "Or I'll fucking kill yer."

"Go away," Aaron shouted. "Go away, Sean."

"Let me in, little man."

Ryan stomped on the last few bugs, but Sean's foul arm still reached through the small window, trying to snatch at them with fingertips of sharpened bone. Brett hurried forward and buried a knife in Sean's forearm. His foul flesh parted like butter, and the blade sliced right down and through the knuckles of Sean's index and middle fingers. His hand and arm split open in a V shape while more bug-infested slurry spilled down the door as Sean roared in agony – a monstrous sound that shouldn't have been possible from human vocal cords. "Yer daft bastards. What you do that for?"

Ryan stomped more bugs, panting as he replied. "Sean, you

need to get out of here. If you try to come inside we're going to hurt you. Do you understand?"

There was silence again for a moment before Sean spoke. "I protected you your entire life, and now you're turning your back on me. You're a Judas, Ryan."

"Just go away, Sean. Please!"

"I ain't going nowhere, our kid. I'm gonna get you. I'm gonna get you all." Ryan screamed as Sean's face appeared in the broken window diamond. His flesh dripped away from his skull, a green and brown slop. Both of his eyes were gone, replaced by writhing insects, his nose a pair of sunken pinholes.

Sean was gone.

A monster had taken his place.

––––––

Sean backed away from the front door, a twisted grin on his unrecognisable face. He spread his arms out to the side as he retreated, almost like the whole thing had been a joke and no harm was intended. Inside the cottage, no one was laughing.

Brett started handing out knives, limping back and forth between them. "He tries to get in here, stab him. That's not our mate out there. Sean's like the rabbit – already dead. We need to make sure the same thing doesn't happen to us."

"He isn't dead," said Aaron. "He was talking to us. It was him."

Ryan nodded. "He was in there. It was him."

Brett picked up a pair of knives from the counter for himself, the two biggest. "He's no different to the cat lying on the road purring, not realising its lower half has been crushed flat by the tyres of a lorry. It might still be alive, but it's temporary. Sean is beyond saving, we all saw it."

Loobey was twirling a wooden-handled steak knife in his hand like he was trying to get used to its weight. "Sean's gone," he said, tears in his eyes. "I'd do anything for it not to be true, but it is. Sean's dead whether he knows it or not, and I didn't suffer months of torment to try and beat cancer only for a fucking fungus to get me. If Sean comes back, I'm planting this in his brain. I'd be doing him a favour."

Ryan collapsed onto the armchair, which was still pushed up against the door. "I can't believe this. We're talking about Sean. He's our mate and he's out there. If there's even a one per cent chance that he can survive this thing, then there's no way I'm going to stab him. Can we just take a minute and think about what we're saying?"

"What if one of *us* gets infected?" said Aaron. "Are we saying we're all prepared to kill each other? Come on!"

"I'm not saying that," said Loobey, "but I'll defend myself if I have to."

"If you *have* too," said Ryan, seizing on the word. "So let's try to avoid that, yeah? Sean is still outside and we're still in here. There's no need to get stab-happy. If we have to go outside, we can probably outrun Sean in the state he's in, so let's focus on that. Killing him doesn't help anything, and what if we find out afterwards that he could have been cured all along? Can we live with that?"

Brett grunted. "Okay, fine. I get your point." He placed the knives back down on the counter and leaned over it, scratching the back of his head. A sigh escaped him and he turned back around. "Look, Ryan, about what I said earlier..."

Ryan waved a hand and dismissed what his friend was about to say. "It don't matter. There are more important things to worry about right now."

"No, really, I'm sorry, Ryan. The truth is that our friendship meant the world to me. I didn't *use* you, and I never expected to grow apart." He chuckled. "Back in the day, I thought we'd be together forever, having barbecues in the garden with our kids and wives. Life seemed easier when we were young, but it's not like that at all. It's tiring and stressful, and it leaves no time for fun. I would love to hang out with the lads every weekend, of course I would, but..."

"But what?"

"But I want a career and a family and a big house in the countryside. I want some land to raise chickens and goats, and maybe even learn how to ride a horse. It might sound silly, but I don't want to feel guilty about wanting those things. I don't want to feel guilty for working hard."

Ryan held up a hand to stop him. "I get it. I don't have the right to tell you what your priorities should be. You can live your life however you want to."

"I just want you to find your own happiness, Ryan. I want you to have the same sense of achievement that I do. I want peace and happiness for you."

"Yeah, I want that too."

Loobey cleared his throat. "What's the deal with Sophie?"

Ryan glanced back towards the front door. The daylight seemed to be dimming already. He checked his watch and saw that it was now past four. How much longer before night fell?

And once again, where the hell was Tom?

Are you okay, mate? Are you dead?

Ryan shivered. He had left his friend's question hanging in the air and Loobey was still waiting for an answer. With a sigh, he tried to avoid giving one. "You really think this is the time to discuss my engagement?"

Loobey shrugged. "It's your stag do. If you don't discuss it now, when will you?"

Brett folded his arms and raised an eyebrow. "Ryan, do you *want* to get married?"

"Yes! Or no. I'm not sure. Sophie is amazing and I love her. In fact, I can't even imagine being with somebody else. Did I ever tell you about how we met?"

Loobey chuckled. "A goose, right?"

Ryan nodded. "Yeah, it started with a goose. That sodding goose."

Brett chuckled. "A goose? I haven't heard this story."

"I was jogging around the lake down by the industrial estate," Ryan began. "You know the one? Well, I must have jogged it a hundred times without a problem, but this one day, it was really hot and I took a break to catch my breath. Next thing I know, this Canada goose comes storming up the embankment like a samurai and attacks me. It's biting my ankles, flapping its wings; seriously, I thought I was gonna die."

Brett erupted into laughter. Loobey was smiling, too, and he clapped his hands in joy. "I love it. Gets me every time."

"Yeah, well, anyway..." Ryan felt his cheeks growing red. "There I am, in a ball on the ground, screaming for dear life, when I hear someone hissing. The goose is honking like a maniac, but slowly it starts to back off. I finally dare to look up and there's this gorgeous brunette staring down at me. She has a rolled-up magazine in her right hand that she used to bat the goose around the head to save me. It was the most embarrassing moment of my life, but she never made me feel silly about it for a moment. I remember her shouting at the goose to "fuck off", like it was a goddamn mugger after my wallet." He shook his head with a smile, remembering it like it was yesterday. "She helped me over to a bench and rubbed my back until I stopped hyperventilating, and then she took me to have a cup of tea for my nerves over at the burger van by the factories. I never went to that sodding lake again, but the rest is history. Sophie literally saved my life that day."

"I doubt the goose would have killed you," said Brett, tears in his eyes from laughing. "It was probably defending its young; they're highly territorial. When you stopped to catch your breath, it must have felt threatened."

"Trust you to take the goose's side," said Ryan. "Anyway, my point is that I've loved Sophie ever since the moment she fought a goose for me."

Brett's laughter disappeared and he appeared confounded. "Then why—"

The front door rattled and Sean peered in at them through the broken window. His eyes were gone, but somehow he seemed to see them anyway. The grin on his face was obscene, and without a word, he reached in through the broken window and let go of something.

A bird took flight, swooping towards Loobey on the sofa. He managed to grab a cushion and shield himself just in time. The bird was tiny but clearly infected by the fungus – a ball of dark green fuzz swooping through the air. A flash of blue might have been the bird's original colouring, but it was no more than a patch.

The bird swooped again, this time aiming for Aaron. Instinctively, Ryan leapt across the room and slapped at it. He missed, but it caused the bird to redirect its flight and miss Aaron. The whole while, Sean cackled with laughter at the broken window. Green fuzz had replaced his eyes, but he knew the peril he had caused them.

Brett slashed at the air with a knife, but the bird was too small and too fast. Several times it almost collided with his face. Loobey batted the bird away with the cushions, screaming like a little girl. It flew silently, making no sound or showing any signs of anger or fear. Yet it was relentless in its aggression, continuously swooping around the room and trying to collide with their terrified faces.

The bird dove at Ryan. Ryan ducked. Ever since the goose attack, he had hated birds, but never had he been afraid of one so small. Would one peck be enough to infect him? One scratch?

Nearby, Aaron scrambled between the sofas and threw himself over to the console table where he grabbed the lamp. The plug pulled away from the socket as he yanked it by the wire and the glowing bulb turned dim.

Brett shouted a warning as the bird swooped around and dove at Ryan a second time. This time, Ryan was already crouched, which left him unable to go lower or move aside. There was no way he could avoid the bird.

Aaron swung the lamp by its cord. Through miraculous luck, or uncanny accuracy, the bulbous lamp base struck the bird in mid-air and knocked it to the ground, where it thudded against the floorboards and started twitching. Immediately, Ryan straightened up and stamped on it, adding its guts to the sloppy mess already coating his trainers. "Pass that on to the goose, you sonofabitch."

Brett hobbled towards the front door with his knife. Despite their earlier conversation, Ryan couldn't bring himself to object. "Sean, if you can hear me – if there's any part of you left – just leave us alone. We won't let you infect us, do you hear me? I'll kill you if I have to."

Still peering in through the broken window diamond, Sean's face distorted, his grin stretching right across his ruined face. Rancid flesh and brown liquid oozed down his cheeks. One of his ears had slid right down onto his collarbone. "It's too late, Brett. It's too late for you."

Brett lunged with the knife, stabbing it through the broken window and trying to sink it into Sean's face. Sean stepped backwards casually and walked away, leaving behind his words.

It's too late for you.

———

"What the hell did he mean?" said Loobey. He began patting himself down, pulling up his sleeves and examining himself. "Are we infected?"

"He's just messing with us," said Brett. "Stay calm."

But Loobey didn't stay calm. "You already said we could breathe it in. What if it's inside me?" He leaned forward on his knees and started taking deep breaths. "I can feel it. It's in my lungs. I can't breathe."

Ryan hurried over and started rubbing his friend's back. "It's all right, Loobs. In and out, slowly, okay? Everything is fine. *You're* fine."

Loobey sucked in air through his nose and let it out through his mouth. "This is so messed up. Seriously, how is this happening? How?"

"Like you said, someone has to be the shit statistic. We're the one in a billion unlucky losers who happened to find a deadly fungus in the middle of nowhere."

"We're definitely going to end up in the newspapers."

"Let's just hope it's not the obituaries."

Brett stood by the front door, peering out of the broken window. After a few moments, he turned around. "Sean's headed off toward the stream. We have to come up with a plan before he comes back."

"We should just make a run for it," said Aaron. "He won't catch us."

Brett held up his swollen ankle. "Speak for yourself."

Aaron groaned. "Oh yeah."

Ryan glanced at his watch. "It's going to start getting dark in an hour or two. If we're going to make a run for it, it would have to be soon. Maybe one of us can go."

"Tom already tried that," said Brett.

"He's dead," said Aaron. "We all know it. The wildlife is infected."

"So are we," muttered Loobey.

"We don't know that," said Brett. He pointed a finger to enforce his point. "Don't make assumptions."

Loobey's eyes went wide, and for a moment it seemed like an overreaction. Then he leaned back against the sofa as if trying to put more space between him and Brett. "Your arm, man! Your arm is green."

Brett was still pointing his finger in the air, but slowly he lowered his eyes to his wrist. Ryan was too far away to see, so he took a step closer. Sure enough, the bottom of Brett's arm had a green circle around it. Several of his fingers were stained as well.

Loobey buried his face in his hands. "Sean was right. It's too late. We're infected."

Aaron lifted his shirt and started checking himself frantically. "I don't see anything on me. Ryan, check my back."

Ryan examined his brother. "You're fine. There's nothing on you. What about me?"

Aaron checked him. "I think you're all right. I don't see anything."

Brett's finger was still piercing the air, but his hand had started to shake. "It's just me," he said, his voice flat and emotionless. "Last night, Sean grabbed my wrist. He grabbed it and held it. I've been infected this entire time." Slowly, he lifted his shirt. Everyone gasped. Green fuzz had grown in half a dozen places. He prodded at it with his fingers. "My skin is numb. That's why I never felt it growing."

Loobey swallowed, the sound loud enough that they all glanced his way. "He grabbed me, too, when he attacked me in the bedroom."

"You were fully clothed," said Ryan. "Did he touch your bare skin anywhere?"

"I... I don't know. I don't think so." Loobey rubbed himself over, prodded at himself, lifted his shirt. "I don't see anything on me. I don't see anything!"

"Then you might be okay," said Ryan.

Brett sat down on the small sofa. He did so mechanically, like he was ordering his limbs to move rather than feeling them. Then he changed his mind. He leapt back up and raced over to the kitchenette's sink, turning on both taps. The bleach was all gone, so he searched for something else, eventually grabbing a fresh bottle of vodka. He poured it into a plastic mixing bowl and submerged his entire hand.

Aaron hurried over to him but kept his distance. "Will alcohol help?"

Brett closed his eyes, his face a picture of pure misery. He ignored the question posed to him, didn't even seem to hear it. "We need to get out of here. I'm not ending up like Sean. I won't!"

Ryan came closer and examined Brett's wrist from a few feet away. A fuzzy green handprint encircled his flesh, an echo of Sean's touch. It confirmed that the infection was spread via contact. "Is there anything I can do?"

"Short of chopping off my hand, no."

Ryan looked at the knives on the counter. None of them looked capable of taking off a hand, but if there was no other choice…

Brett's expression turned sour. "I was joking. No one is cutting off my hand. I just need to get to a hospital. That's what you can do for me. Get me in front of a doctor who understands this, because I sure as hell don't."

"No problem," said Ryan, not knowing what else to say. "I'll get you to a doctor. I promise."

"Give over!" Brett always worked hard to keep his speech polite and educated, but more and more the Manchester boy was escaping. "It's ain't like we can catch a bus. I can't get anywhere on this sodding ankle."

"I can't make it into the village either," said Loobey. "I'll be out of breath before I make it halfway. Less, if Sean legs it after us."

"Either we all go or none of us do," said Ryan, "so where does that leave us?"

"What if we try rolling Tom's car?" Aaron suggested. "We're uphill, right? Maybe, if we can get the car to the road, we can roll it all the way into the village."

Brett seemed to mull it over, and then shrugged. "Even if it gets us halfway, it would help."

"We still have to make it inside the car," said Loobey. "Sean's still out there, along with God knows how many infected animals."

"You're right," said Brett, "but what's the alternative? Ryan, when does the landlord expect you back with the keys?"

"He said he would come by Sunday, around noon."

Brett grimaced, glancing back at Loobey. "You see? We can't wait until tomorrow. Who knows what Sean will dump through the window next? Not to mention..." He held up his wrist. Tiny green hairs had begun to sprout from the oily stain. "Time is literally ticking for me, Loobey. I don't have the option of staying put."

Loobey nodded unhappily. "Then I guess we're making a run for the car."

Brett grabbed a knife from the counter. "I'm already infected, so I'll lead the way."

Ryan disagreed. "You might be infected, but that doesn't mean you can't get hurt. We stick together the whole way. Mates, right?"

Brett nodded. "Yeah, mates. I'd shake your hand, but..."

"Yeah, stay the fuck away from me." Ryan smiled to show he was joking. Sean might be beyond help, but he was going to do whatever he could to help Brett. There had to be a way out of all of this. It couldn't be as bad as it seemed.

This all has to make sense somehow. It's 2020, not the Dark Ages. Doctors can treat everything.

Aaron looked towards the door. "Should we make a plan first?"

"It's going to get dark," said Ryan. "There's no way we'll be able to find our way back to the village in the dark. Even in the car, we'd lose the road and end up in a ditch. The odds are the same whatever time we leave, so we might as well get it over with. The plan is to run for the car and get in as quickly as we can."

"Wait?" said Brett. "Do we even have keys?"

Ryan patted his pockets, even though he knew he didn't have them. The only keys in his pocket were those the landlord had given him, a small bundle on a Scottish flag keyring, along with his own personal car keys. "Tom must have them. Damn it."

"It's unlocked," said Loobey. "Brett and I were checking the engine earlier, remember? The driver's door is still unlocked from when Tom opened it last night manually with the key. The auto locking is as dead as the engine."

"What about the other doors?" asked Ryan.

Loobey shrugged. "Never checked 'em. Hopefully they will be."

Ryan moved over to the front door and peered out of the broken window. "I don't see Sean. No animals either. Are we ready to do this?"

"No," said Loobey, "and that ain't gonna change." He pulled himself up off the sofa, stretched and flexed. "But what choices do we have?"

Ryan sighed. "None."

"Then let's go."

Ryan placed his hand on the door handle.

CHAPTER NINE

Everyone put on their coats and gathered at the door, none of them happy. Ryan checked his watch. The sun was going to start setting soon. They had to do this now or they would be trapped inside the cottage until morning. As he clutched the door handle, Ryan wondered if he was making contact with the fungus. Brett had said it could live on almost any surface. Had Brett touched the door handle? Had Sean?

Sean let himself out this morning. His hand must have touched the handle.

Aaron looked at him. "You all right, Ryan?"

"Yeah, just taking a minute. Everyone ready?"

They all nodded.

"Then let's begin." Ryan opened the front door and hurried out onto the gravel driveway. There he stood, searching left and right. No sign of Sean or the animals. Tom's car was still parked nearby. The coast was clear.

Ryan turned back and grabbed Brett, despite his protests, and helped him to walk. He winced with every step, but they had no choice but to move quickly. Each second was a hypodermic needle injecting more and more anxiety into Ryan's veins. Sean must be out there somewhere, watching them, stalking them. He wouldn't have just walked away. His promise to kill them had seemed too genuine.

In a group, they hurried towards the car, their footsteps unavoidably crunching on the gravel. The Stelvio's sleek bonnet was still propped up, so Ryan told Loobey to drop it. He did as he was asked, knocking away the prop and letting the lid dropped down with a loud *clonk*. Everyone winced.

"You idiot!" Ryan said through gritted teeth.

Loobey blushed. "Sorry, our kid."

Shaking his head, Ryan grabbed the driver's side door handle. Mercifully, the door opened without argument. He quickly bundled Brett inside, glad to be free from the burden of his weight. Aaron dodged by him and tried the rear passenger door. The handle sprung out but the door stayed shut. "It's locked."

"Damn it."

Loobey moved to the other side of the car and tried the front passenger door. "Same here. Brett, lean over and pull the—"

Ryan registered movement from an unexpected place. He looked upwards, expecting to see a bird, but instead he saw Sean, crouched on the high-pitched roof that sheltered the front door. His legs straddled the peak on either side. His face had now fallen away completely, leaving behind a bare brown-stained skull. Both his eyes were balls of green fuzz. His mouth was an empty maw, barely any teeth remaining. Ryan tried to grab Loobey, but the bonnet was between them. "Loobey, move!"

Loobey clearly had no idea why Ryan was shouting, but the urgency was enough to communicate danger. He leapt back from the car, knowing only that he needed to be somewhere else. It was enough to move him out of harm's way.

Sean came crashing down against the side of the car's bonnet, fists thumping into the painted steel and making two deep dents. When Loobey realised his near miss, he staggered back on his heels, moving away from Sean as fast as he could.

Then he tripped and fell.

Sean turned and opened his skeletal jaws, releasing a cascade of soaking wet bugs.

Not thinking, Ryan leapt onto the bonnet and used the added height to kick Sean's lumpen skull like a soccer ball. He might have been a monster, but the ferocious impact was enough to send him sprawling on the gravel driveway. Wasting no time, Ryan raced to the other side of the car and gathered Loobey to his feet. "Come on, mate, get in the car."

Brett was already reaching over to unlock the passenger door, and when Ryan yanked on the handle, it opened. He got Loobey inside and slammed the door, before searching for his brother. Aaron was yanking at the rear handle, yelling at Brett to let him in.

Sean leapt back on his feet. Somehow his arms had elongated and now ended with single sharp talons. There was no time to wait for Loobey or Brett to clamber over the seats and unlock the rear doors. Sean would be on them in seconds.

Ryan took a step in the direction of the cottage's front door, but Sean dashed in front of him, seeing him through the fuzzy masses filling his eye sockets. Ryan took another step, and once again Sean matched it. He turned to his brother. "Aaron, get the hell out of here. I'll keep him busy."

"No way. I'm not going without you."

Ryan grunted and looked desperately around. He took in the ominous cross and the white stones. Next, he took in the juddering generator, peeking out from behind the shed. Then he took in the shed itself. He felt the weight of the landlord's keys in his pocket. He fished them out and tossed them to Aaron. "The shed! Get inside the shed."

Aaron took off just as Sean attacked. He leapt at Ryan, slicing at his face with one of those sharp talons. His arms were more like lengths of spongy elastic now, rather than anything with bone and muscle. The talon whipped through the air like a striking cobra.

Ryan ducked, the talon disturbing the air a few centimetres from his head. From down low he scooped up a handful of gravel – groaning when he saw it filled with writhing bugs – and tossed it in Sean's face. The bugs went airborne, scattering over the driveway. Instead of attacking again, Sean turned and watched the critters fall.

Ryan bolted for the shed, praying that the bundle of keys the landlord had given him contained one for the shed – and that Aaron could find it and get inside in time to keep them from being infected.

Mam is definitely going to kill me.

Aaron was at the shed's door, struggling with a large brass

padlock. Ryan reached his side, gasping for air. "Do you have the right key? Do you?" He glanced back at Sean, who had finished checking on the welfare of the bugs and was once again focused on attacking them. "Aaron?"

"Hold on, hold on, I'm trying." Aaron had about six keys to deal with. He was trying them one after another, but each failed attempt led to a wasted second of jangling the key and trying to get it unstuck from the lock. He was taking too long.

Sean began to stagger along the driveway, picking up speed. Bugs spilled from his open mouth. His talons whipped the air like monstrous tentacles. He was completely silent as he approached.

Ryan grabbed his brother's arm. "Come on, we need to get out of here."

"One second. There's only one more key."

"There's no time. Come on!"

Sean leaned forward and sprinted towards the shed. Even if Aaron found the right key, there was no time to unlock the door and get inside. Ryan raised his fists, knowing that a barehanded fight would definitely infect him but seeing no other way to protect his brother.

"I've got it," said Aaron, but it was too late. Way too late.

Sean raised a talon, preparing to strike.

"Hey, Sean, watch this!"

Loobey had got back out of the car. He started tap-dancing on the gravel, a picture of ridiculousness. He was squashing the bugs that had fallen around the car.

Sean skidded to a halt, gravel spraying up in the air. He let out an ear-piercing scream and turned around, then ran back towards the car – towards Loobey.

What the hell are you doing, our kid?

Loobey continued tap-dancing for another second, then stopped. He glared at Sean, as angry as Ryan had ever seen him. "I'm sorry, Sean, but I don't think we can be bessies any more."

Sean leapt at Loobey, but Loobey quickly slid back inside the car and slammed the door. Clearly enraged, Sean whipped his talons at the window over and over again, but the glass didn't break.

"Ryan, come on!" Aaron grabbed his brother from behind and yanked him backwards into darkness.

———

The shed was dark, but not pitch-black due to a small amount of light spilling in through a plastic window at the rear. Ryan searched for a light switch but couldn't find one. Then Aaron yanked on a pull cord and a naked bulb came to life above their heads, hanging from a cobweb-covered wire.

Ryan needed to know that Loobey was okay, but there was no way to see what was happening outside. There were no windows or openings facing the driveway. He had seen Loobey make it back inside the car, but was that enough to keep him safe from Sean? How long before Sean managed to break the window with those talons of his?

Talons? He's turned into a monster.

This isn't just a fungus.

Ryan checked his hands and wrists underneath the lightbulb, expecting to see green stains. So far, he could find nothing. How long would it take for the infection to show? How long did Brett have?

"They're trapped in the car," said Ryan, "and we're trapped in here. Things are even worse than before."

"Maybe not," said Aaron. "Take a look around you."

Ryan realised he was panting, so he concentrated on calming his breathing. Once his lungs were under control, he did as his brother asked and looked around. The shed was crammed full of tools, equipment, and random junk. A petrol mower and a chainsaw were secured by a rope to the wall opposite the window, and beneath the window was a workbench stocked with an all manner of tools. In addition, there was a rusty old barbecue and a pair of mountain bikes.

"This could be our way out of here," said Aaron, clutching the handlebars of one of the bicycles and lifting it upright. Both of them seemed in good shape – a little faded and old-fashioned, but no rust and all four tyres were inflated.

"What, you want to go cycling through the Highlands?"

Aaron huffed. "Yes! We can race to the edge of the hill and then coast all the way down. There's no way Sean will be able to catch us."

"Did you see Sean? Hell, that thing ain't even him any more. It's a monster, and it leapt off that roof like a goddamn gorilla. If we try and make a run for it, it'll be on top of us before we make it past the driveway. I don't fancy trying our luck."

"It's an alien," said Aaron.

"Come on…"

"I'm telling you, it's an alien. How can you even deny it? There's nothing natural that can change a person like that. The corkscrew came from space."

Ryan wanted to argue. If he had an alternative theory, he would have put it forward, but the truth was that he had no idea what was happening aside from the fact it was horrifying and unbelievable. Sean had gone from man to monster in a single weekend. It didn't take a doctor to see how wrong that was.

"I don't know what this is, Aaron, but mam made me promise to keep you safe, so, somehow, I need to get us out of here. I don't think a pair of old mountain bikes is going to cut it."

"What about this then?" Aaron nodded at the chainsaw.

Ryan had never used a chainsaw before, but he suddenly pictured himself revving the thing up and slicing Sean to pieces. It was an unpleasant image, yet strangely empowering. He lifted the tool from behind the rope holding it in place. "I just pull this cord, right?"

"Don't ask me."

Ryan huffed. "Okay, well, here goes." He yanked at a small plastic loop attached to a nylon cord, turning his head away and wincing. Nothing happened. He yanked the cord again, several times, but all he managed to produce was a weak, throaty sound from the tool's inner workings. Defeated, he hoisted the chainsaw and rattled it beside his head. "I think it's out of petrol. Is there any in here? They must keep some for the generator."

Both brothers searched, but it didn't take them long to discover that there wasn't any petrol lying around inside the shed. Ryan swore in disappointment.

"We could syphon it from Tom's car?" Aaron suggested.

"If we could safely go outside and syphon petrol, we wouldn't need the sodding chainsaw, would we?"

Aaron tutted and turned away, rooting through the various junk in search of a solution.

Ryan sighed. "Sorry, I'm just on edge – obviously. I keep expecting to wake up from this nightmare, but it keeps on going. Did I take some of Sean's gear last night?"

"No, but it probably would have been better if you had. This whole thing is like a drug trip – not that I'd know." He shared a laugh with himself, then muttered, "I should have stayed at home."

Ryan was hurt for a second, but then he leaned back against the wooden slats making up the walls and let out a long sigh. "I shouldn't have dragged you up here."

"Why did you? Why did you even want me here, Ryan?"

"You having a laugh? You're my little bro – of course I wanted you here. Cartwright brothers united, yeah?"

"United until one of them goes and gets married."

Ryan groaned. "You really want me to stay at home forever?"

"Yes!"

Petulance was a natural defence for a fifteen-year-old, but it still managed to aggravate, and Ryan groaned at the display of selfishness. Aaron seemed to realise he was being unfair, because he quickly apologised. "Of course I don't expect you to stay at home just for me, but I thought you would take a little more time before you upped and left. Why can't you wait a while longer before you marry Sophie?"

"Because I love her!" Ryan almost shouted it, a sudden need to defend his choices taking over him. He had asked Sophie to marry him because he loved her, that much he knew. His reluctance had only arrived afterwards, as the wedding drew nearer, but on the night he had popped the question there had been no doubt in his mind. He had wanted to marry Sophie.

I wanted it more than anything else in the world.

It had happened at Alton Towers. They were riding Oblivion, suspended in mid-air and waiting to plummet into the smoky depths below. Ryan had been terrified, sure he was going to die, so he had reached out and grabbed Sophie's hand. They fell and he screamed, but he never let go of her hand. A moment later, they emerged from a dark tunnel and whipped back into the light – safe and alive and deliriously happy. Right then was the moment Ryan had known with his entire being that the woman laughing beside him was the most important thing in his life, and that he wanted to spend decades sharing moments like this with her. Scary moments. Funny moments. Sad moments. He didn't want any of it if it wasn't with her.

Ryan had asked Sophie to marry him the moment they stepped off the ride. It wasn't romantic or thoughtful, but it was real. Sophie must have felt the authenticity of his proposal because she had said yes. She had said yes, and a week later they were picking out rings.

Then the fear had set in.

"I know you love her," said Aaron, "but it just seems like you're rushing things."

Ryan stepped in front of his brother and placed a hand on his shoulder. "I've been with Sophie for eighteen months, but you're right, it's not that long. The thing is, though, when you fall in love, it only takes a second. If it takes any longer than that then you're not doing it right." Aaron tried to turn away, but Ryan wouldn't let him. "I love Sophie, and I'm going to marry her as soon as I get the hell away from this cottage, but you know what, little brother? Nothing will ever replace my love for you. Till the day I die, I'll always be your big brother; I'll always have your back; but I need you to have my back too. I need you to be a man and be happy for me. Be happy for me because I'm finally moving forward with my life."

Aaron seemed angry for a moment, but slowly he softened. Tears formed in his eyes, but he hid them by pulling Ryan into a hug. "I am happy for you. I'm just sad for me. That's okay, though, because you're right – it's time for me to grow up. It's time for me to get out from under your shadow and see what life's all about."

Ryan eased out of the hug, a smile on his face. "We're going to get out of here, Aaron. We're going to get out of here and take life by the balls, yeah?"

Aaron wiped a tear from his face and smiled. "Yeah, but no matter what, we don't tell mam about any of this."

"Too bloody right!"

———

The shaft of light coming in through the plastic window diluted more and more. The sun was deserting them and it would soon be dark outside. Ryan found himself standing directly beneath the dangling lightbulb in the centre of the shed, as if its glow might keep him safe. Aaron was standing near the back, readying the two bicycles that he still insisted were their best way out of the situation. He was probably right. It would sure beat running.

Ryan looked towards the shed door, wishing he could see through it. How long had they been hiding in there now? An hour? Two? "Do you think Brett and Loobey are okay?"

"I don't know." Aaron's glum tone suggested he thought not. Sean was still out there somewhere.

They had armed themselves as best they could after having searched the shed's inventory, and Ryan now held a sixteen-ounce hammer. Its wooden handle was old and splintered, but the tool was solid overall. It would break bone. Aaron held a pitchfork with only three tines, the left-middle one snapped away. It would have to do.

"This one has a light," said Aaron, switching on a small torch mounted to the handlebars of one of the bikes. The frame was yellow, while the other bike was red. "We're going to have to make a break for it eventually."

Ryan didn't want to think about it. Out there, in the night-covered hills, the ground would be merciless. Arriving by daylight in a four-by-four had been hazardous enough. Mr McGregor knew the roads but had still taken every corner cautiously while bringing them up here.

The lightbulb overhead flickered, causing both brothers to glance at each other. Aaron pulled a face. "How long do you think the generator will last?"

"McGregor said it would last all weekend. He said the solar panels supplied most of the power and the generator was just a backup."

Aaron's eyes widened. "The solar panels? Shit, they were probably fried by the EMP. If they were…"

Ryan groaned. "Then the generator will be working overtime and we might not have long left."

The lightbulb flickered again.

Ryan grabbed his hair with both hands. "I can't stay here in the dark, man. I'll go to pieces."

Aaron shushed him. "It'll be all right. Don't panic."

"I feel trapped. It's almost worse than being outside with Sean."

"It's not and you know it. We're safe in here. Keep your head and we'll figure a way out of this."

Ryan nodded. He wasn't usually claustrophobic, but these were extreme circumstances. Being trapped inside an old spider-infested shed, miles from anywhere, and with a monster stalking them was enough to make anyone panic. In fact, he was surprised by how calm Aaron was being.

He's been calm all along. I don't give the kid enough credit.

The light in the room shifted as something moved past the plastic window and cast a weak shadow. A subtle sound, like crumpling paper, caught their attention. Aaron took a step to see what was happening. His expression left no doubt that it was bad. "Bugs! They're coming in through the window."

Ryan didn't dare move closer, but he spotted a tiny gap between the plastic window and the wood. Bugs were scuttling through, one by one, like fat-legged slugs. Ryan looked at the hammer in his hand, reassured by the weight. "I think we should make a break for it. If we have any chance, we need to go while there's a tiny bit of sunlight left, and I'd rather face Sean than stay in here with all these bugs."

Aaron seemed pained, but he nodded. "I don't think we have a choice. Once the light goes out, we'll have no way of seeing where the bugs are. We'll get infected. I swear, if we make it back to the village, I'm coming right back with a flamethrower."

"I won't argue with that, but listen to me, Aaron, okay? If Sean is out there, leave him to me. I'm your big brother, which means I'm the one who takes the risks."

Aaron rolled his eyes.

"I ain't kidding. Once we get outside, you get on a bike and pedal like crazy. Anything else, you leave to me. I need you to promise me. Promise me!"

Aaron shrugged. "Whatever, I promise. Can we just get out of here before we're covered in bugs?"

"All right."

By now the bugs had started to drop onto the floor beneath the window. Aaron stamped on a few, but they kept on coming. It was now or never.

Ryan stepped out of the bulb's weak halo and went to the shed's door. It was on a latch but not locked, which filled Ryan with horror that he hadn't done anything to secure it. In his panic, he hadn't even thought about it. As it turned out, the monster outside had made no attempt to get in. Was it unable to physically? Or hadn't it even occurred to it to try and open the door?

Sean would have known how to get inside. He would have grabbed the handle. Does that mean he's truly gone?

Yeah. He's been gone a while.

He's gone.

Ryan felt a hitch in his throat, and he had to push aside his feelings before he broke down. He placed his left hand on the shed's handle and held the hammer in his right. His thumb moved to the latch release. His heart pounded in his chest.

"Wait," said Aaron, then he wheeled both bicycles to the front of the shed. He propped one against the wall, but the other – the yellow one with the light – he straddled, ready to take off. "You gonna get on the other bike?"

"Soon as I open the door. After three, okay? One... two... three!"

Ryan pressed the latch release and pushed the door outwards and stepped onto the driveway.

Where's Sean?

Ryan searched left and right and caught movement over by the car. It wasn't what he expected though, and instead of seeing Sean, he saw Loobey throwing himself onto the driveway. He hit the gravel and immediately started scrambling, fear igniting a fire behind him.

Ryan called out. "Loobey!"

Loobey looked up and saw Ryan, and it caused him to change direction. He straightened up and sprinted towards the shed. "Run," he shouted. "It's Brett."

"What do you mean?" Aaron shook his head in confusion. Instead of taking off on his bike, he chose to stand idly by. When Loobey reached the brothers, Aaron asked the question again. "What do you mean about Brett?"

Loobey grabbed Aaron and shook him. "Get the hell out of here."

Ryan grabbed the other bicycle from inside the shed and rolled it towards Loobey. "Take it. Get Aaron to the village."

Loobey took the handlebars, thought about it, then rolled the bicycle back. "No, man. Brothers should stick together. You go with Aaron. I'll never make it. I'm too weak."

There was a loud *crack* from the car. Everyone turned around.

A bony arm broke through the driver's side window, brown flesh melting away and dripping onto the driveway. Bugs erupted from a bony protrusion on the back of a rotting hand.

Loobey put his palm over his mouth and wobbled. "That's what I mean about Brett. He's changed. Like Sean. Only worse."

Ryan swallowed a hot coal in his throat. "How could he be worse?"

Loobey shoved the bicycle at Ryan. "You don't want to stick around to find out."

CHAPTER TEN

A aron was on the yellow bike, ready to ride away. The problem was who took the red bike. No way would Ryan take off and leave Loobey behind, but it seemed like Loobey was in the same mind frame. He waved a hand at Ryan. "Go, Ryan, now!"

"I'm not leaving you."

"Me neither," said Aaron. "Take my bike. I'll run."

"This isn't a video game. You'll be out of breath before you make it a hundred metres."

"He's right," said Ryan. "I've seen you on sports day."

Brett was still inside the car, his bony arm hanging out of the broken window. He was shouting at them, but the raspy voice was alien. It didn't sound like Brett at all. "A little help... A little help here, please? Hey, Ryan? Be a mate and help me. Be a mate and help me."

Ryan took a step towards the car, but Loobey put a hand on his chest. "That ain't him in there, man. Trust me."

As if to prove a point, Brett shoved his head and shoulder through the car window. He was facing away, but the back of his head was elongated and misshapen, more like a hairy peanut shell than a human skull. Slowly, like a slimy octopus, he pushed more and more of himself through the small gap, until eventually his entire body flopped onto the driveway like a stillborn foetus.

Ryan felt woozy, his legs getting weak beneath him. "Brett?"

"Get on the goddamn bikes," Loobey shouted.

Fear made Ryan selfish, and he finally jumped onto the red bike's saddle. Rather than complain, Loobey put a hand on each of their backs and shoved. "I'll hide in the shed," he said. "Bring help."

Ryan didn't have chance to reply. Movement to his right caught all of their attention. It came from the cross beside the cottage. Perching on the cross beam, and lit by the last gasps of sunset, Sean glared at them like a twisted bird of prey. The white stones on the ground below him were stained green.

Sean raced towards them, taking them by surprise. The resulting collision knocked Ryan clean off his bike and onto his back. Sean whipped one of his talons like a cowboy's whip. Ryan threw an arm out and wailed as a white-hot flash of agony bit into his elbow. He rolled aside, desperate to get out of danger, and grabbed at his aching elbow. In his horror, he expected to see blood, but he was monumentally relieved when he saw his coat still intact. The talon had struck him hard, but it hadn't made it through to his skin – more a vicious punch than a slice.

Sean whipped his talon again but missed. Ryan cried out for help, almost calling for his mam. It took him back to when the ex-paratrooper had knocked him unconscious and broken his arm, and just like then, Aaron was once again a fearful spectator. The fun had turned deadly once more.

Forgive me, brother.

Loobey tackled Sean to the ground. In his current, emaciated form, Sean was only one third of Loobey's size, and he was unable to get out from under him once he was pinned to the ground. He whipped his talons and thrashed, but he couldn't get free. Loobey sprawled himself out, making himself even heavier.

At the same time, Brett stood up on the driveway. He was at least two feet taller than before, but inhumanely thin, as if a cruel God had clutched him by the head and feet before stretching him out. His fuzzy green eyes were uneven, the left at least an inch lower than the right. In the centre of his face only part of his nose remained. In a matter of hours, Brett had transformed.

He tottered towards them now, like some kind of humanoid plant. His arm waved wildly like a plant stem, like the bones inside had turned to liquid. He hadn't yet formed the talons that had replaced Sean's arms, but several of his fingers had fallen away to make way for the emerging bone.

Not bone. Chitin.

It really is aliens. Sean and Brett have been taken over by aliens.

Aaron stood next to Ryan, brandishing his pitchfork. "We have to do this, right? That isn't Brett any more. Or Sean?"

"I really wish you would get on that bike and leave, little brother."

"You think I want to survive if it means leaving you here to die? You think I could ever forgive myself for that? No way. We get out of this together or not at all."

Ryan glanced at Aaron and saw a stranger. He saw a man. "Looks like you're all grown up. I'm proud."

"I had a great big brother as a role model."

Brett came for them, swiping his arms but unable to use them fully yet – the last remnants of bone making them too rigid to whip. There was an inhuman quality to his gaze as he glared at Ryan, even as he spoke. "Your life is behind you, Ryan. All that's left is the drudgery of growing old."

Ryan swallowed, dreading that the words were coming from Brett. Were these his genuine beliefs, or was the fungus messing with his brain? The answer quickly became apparent. "That's not Brett talking. Brett spent his whole childhood looking ahead. He couldn't wait to grow up. Life was finally exactly how he wanted it, and you took it away from him. Brett, if you're still in there, you were always the best of us – and I love you, man."

Ryan and Aaron raced forward at the same time. Ryan swung his hammer at Brett's misshapen skull, catching him in the temple while Aaron buried his three-tined pitchfork underneath his twisted ribcage. Flesh parted like butter. Bone shattered like eggshell. Brett screeched, a torrent of blood and brown fluid erupting from his foul jaws. Bugs slopped onto the ground alongside liquidised viscera. Aaron twisted the pitchfork and opened up a deep hole in Brett's stomach. More bugs emerged from the gaping wound, falling onto the driveway. Immediately, a dark green stain started spreading throughout the gravel. They were ejecting the infectious oil.

Ryan pried his hammer out of the sticky brown hole he had left in his friend's skull and swung it again. This time he planted the hammer right in the middle of Brett's forehead. His skull parted, opening up to reveal chunks of decaying brain matter. The brown ooze spilled between the cracked bone and dripped down Brett's ruined face. His body collapsed onto the driveway, Aaron's pitchfork still buried in his guts. Aaron yanked it free and planted it in the mush that was the remains of Brett's head. The last of it came apart.

Ryan bent over and vomited.

Still battling with Sean on the ground, Loobey cried out for help.

———

Loobey was losing his grip, and it was clear why. Sweat came from his every pore, the exertion far too much for his diminished reserves. Sean already had half his body free, lashing out with one of his tendrils and whipping it back and forth in the air. Loobey did his best to avoid the talon on the end.

Aaron retrieved his pitchfork from Brett's skull and quickly came to Loobey's aid. He planted the tines in the gravel, pinning Sean's tendril underneath. It was just in time, too, because Loobey finally gave in, rolling aside and gasping for breath.

Sean was finally free of Loobey's weight.

Ryan lunged with his hammer, attempting to plant it in the middle of Sean's forehead – erasing whatever was left of his friend – but he was caught by surprise as an unpinned tendril whipped at the hammer and knocked it from his grasp. Instinctively, Aaron pulled his pitchfork free from the ground, causing him to unwittingly free Sean's other tendril. Now unrestrained, Sean leapt to his feet. His skeletal face had cracked apart on one side, bugs scuttling out of the bony chasm.

Ryan turned and dragged Loobey to his feet. "Look, we need to go."

"Can't."

Aaron thrust at Sean with the pitchfork, but Sean's tendril lashed out and wrapped around the metal shaft. Aaron fought to hold onto it, but the pitchfork was quickly torn from his grasp. "Shit! We need to make a run for it."

Ryan attempted to grab one of the bicycles lying on the ground, but Sean leapt in the way. He whipped both tendrils at the same time, trying to scissor Ryan in half, but he was able to lunge out of the way just in time. He spotted his hammer lying on the driveway and tried to make a grab for it, but once again Sean moved in the way. The monster was too fast, its whip-like appendages slicing through the air.

Loobey appeared and grabbed Ryan, but his grasp was weak, almost childlike. "Go, Ryan, please. You have to get help." Ryan went to argue, but Loobey shoved him. "It's too late for me."

Aaron tried to get around behind Sean, edging slowly towards his fallen pitchfork. Sean saw the movement and lashed out at him, almost slicing his throat. The near miss filled Ryan with dread. He had to get his little brother out of there.

Ryan looked at Loobey. "We can't leave you. I can't leave you to die."

"I'm already dead." Loobey held up his arm. The back of his hand was sliced right open, blood flowing down the woollen sleeve of his coat. Mixed with the blood were tiny splotches of green. "Sean got me. Always said he'd be the death of me."

"You're not dying."

"Yeah, mate, I am. I was dying before this weekend even got started."

Ryan understood immediately. He had known Loobey too long not to sense the tone in his voice. "Your cancer is worse than you let on."

Loobey nodded.

Nearby, Sean continued hunting Aaron. Ryan was desperate to go save him, but...

Loobey... He's my best friend.

"I'm sorry I lied to you, Ryan. I didn't want to ruin your stag do, but there was no way I could miss it either. Just get out of here, okay? Get help. It's your only option."

Ryan turned and grabbed the pair of bicycles, propping them upright. He turned to Loobey and smiled, doing everything he could to keep his tears at bay. "Don't worry about it, our kid. We all knew Sean would be the one to blame if this weekend turned bad."

"Yeah, he really fucked things up this time, huh?"

Aaron wheeled his way back around towards Ryan, ducking and dodging with surprising dexterity. "I guess those video games finally paid off, little brother. Crash Bandicoot would be proud."

Aaron frowned. "Who?"

"Never mind, we're getting out of here."

"What about Loobey?"

Loobey started backing up towards the shed. "Don't worry about me. I'm gonna stick around, clean up a bit." Aaron frowned, but before he could say anything, Loobey started shouting at Sean, waving his arms around like a madman. "Hey, Sean, come give your old mate a hug. That's it, come on."

Sean's green-fuzzed eyes fixated on Loobey, as if attracted by the movement. Or was it the noise getting his attention? Either way, Ryan and Aaron stood completely still while Loobey danced and shouted. Eventually, he got all of Sean's attention. "We always said you'd catch something one of these days, yer mad bastard. We just assumed it'd be the clap. Come on, you Manc twat. Let's see how hard you are!"

Sean made no sound as he rushed furiously at Loobey. Loobey retreated backwards, heading towards the open door of the shed. Ryan wanted to do something, to try and grab the hammer in time to save his friend, but it was too late.

Loobey took a few more steps and then Sean leapt at him, tendrils whipping in the air. Loobey threw out his arms and wrapped them around Sean's emaciated waist, pulled him into a tight embrace. They tumbled, together, towards the shed. Loobey turned, forcing Sean through the open doorway as they fell. Before he disappeared, he managed to reach out and pull on the door handle.

The door slammed shut.

Silence.

Behind the shed, the generator conked out with an asthmatic grunt. The last of the sun disappeared. Inside the shed, Loobey was alone with Sean, in the dark. His grunts of exertion turned into agonised screams.

Aaron stepped towards the shed, but Ryan grabbed the back of his jacket. "Loobey's gone. You might not understand it, but he's gone. We need to get out of here."

"But—"

Ryan picked up a bike and thrust it towards Aaron. "You said it yourself, someone needs to come here with a flamethrower."

A single tear spilled down Aaron's cheek, but he nodded.

The brother's Cartwright mounted their bikes and pedalled away. The stag do was over.

———

Aaron rode the yellow bike and led the way with his light. As soon as they made it down to the stream, they saw how bad things were. A fox glared at them, but only one of its eyes shone beneath the newborn moon. The other was a shadowy fuzz. Several times, rabbits bolted towards them, but their coordination was poisoned by the fungus and Ryan and Aaron were able to skirt by them. It felt like the infection was all around them, growing out of the very earth. How quickly did the green oil spread? Had all of the wildlife caught it from the corkscrew on the hill?

What the hell is that thing? Where did it come from?

Ryan had to keep telling himself to slow down. He wanted nothing more than to feel the wind in his hair as he put more and more distance between him and the cottage, but the night had gone from grey to black, and every curve in the road hid a pothole, rock, or precipice. One wrong turn and he could be lying out in the open with a broken leg. Aaron, too, was pushing his luck, and several times his front wheel had hit an obstacle and caused him to wobble frantically until he regained his balance.

After a while, it felt safe enough to slow down, so Ryan called ahead to get Aaron to pump the pedals a little less hard. They settled into a new rhythm, side by side, but neither of them spoke for a long while. Eventually, Aaron broke the silence. "We shouldn't have left Loobey behind. He wouldn't have done that to us."

"He was infected," said Ryan between gasps. "Not only that, but he was dying from cancer."

Aaron turned sideways. "What?"

"He was dying of cancer. None of us knew it, but this weekend was his goodbye. I don't think he had long."

The silence resumed for a few minutes more until Aaron spoke again. "Loobey was really dying?"

"I swear down. He was infected too. Back at the cottage, he showed me his arm. Sean had got him. One slice of those talons and it's game over, I think. It's a miracle we got out of there alive. Brett... Brett wasn't so lucky."

"He changed so fast."

"He'd been infected for a while. I just think it was happening on the inside. We never noticed until it was too late."

They sped around a bend in the narrow road and then descended a dip. Ryan's tummy fluttered and he found it comforting. A normal bodily function that told him he was alive. Or were his insides teeming with fungus? Brett had had no idea. He hadn't known he was changing.

As if thinking the same thing, Aaron said, "Brett changed much quicker than Sean did."

"You're right."

"Maybe it was all the drugs he took. The fungus might not like to get high."

Ryan was too numb to laugh immediately, but after a second, a cackle erupted from his lips. "Even a deadly fungus couldn't keep up with Sean. God bless him."

"No way is he getting an invite to Heaven."

Ryan's cackle became a chuckle. "Yeah, he'll probably have more fun in Hell anyway."

"I'm going to miss him."

"Me too."

They rode on for another half a mile, but this time they didn't do so in silence. They chatted and chuckled, glad to be free of the terror. A numbness had set in, pressing pause on the horror they had witnessed, and it allowed them to think about something else. For now, they had a task, and that task was riding to the village to get help. The mental breakdowns could come later. The mourning and therapy could wait.

At least I still have my brother.

"I need to speak to Sophie," said Ryan, realising how glad he was that he would get to see her again. "She's going to be going out of her mind with worry. She's probably been thinking strippers, though, not green fungus monsters."

Aaron chuckled, but it was a tense sound. "No one is going to believe us. When we tell them what happened, they're going to lock us up in a looney bin."

"You're probably right, but when we tell them our friends are dead up at the cottage, they'll have no choice but to investigate. They'll see what happened. Then it's their problem."

"They're all dead," said Aaron, disbelief in his voice. "They're really gone, aren't they?"

Ryan didn't give an answer. It was too painful to say out loud.

Another minute's ride took them to the bottom of a hill. The village wasn't far away now. In fact, they passed by a gutted, weed-covered outbuilding that Ryan remembered passing on the ride up to the cottage. That ride felt like a lifetime ago.

"There's something in the road," said Aaron. "I think it's a car."

Ryan squinted to see in the dark. The light on Aaron's bike was weak, but there was most certainly a car up ahead, a Land Rover or other large vehicle. It was parked off to the side of the road, it lights and engine switched off. Ryan took a hand off the handlebars and checked his watch. It was just passed eight – an odd time to be parked in the middle of the nowhere. "Slow down, Aaron."

Aaron did as he was told, coasting without peddling. After a dozen or so metres, they both stopped and got off their bikes, choosing to walk beside them. Ryan risked a glance back behind them, wondering how close the nearest infected animal was. How many birds had taken flight with the fungus coating their wings?

We'll be able to deal with this. Whatever it is, we'll find a way to cure it – or kill it – or burn it. It's just a fungus.

A fungus from outer space.

The car's driver side door was hanging wide open. Once Ryan got closer, he saw it was an old Land Rover. One he recognised.

"Mr McGregor?"

"Mr Cartwright?"

Ryan and Aaron jolted, instinctively pressing against one another. The voice had come from the rear of the Land Rover, and as they looked, a shadowy figure stepped out into the dim light cast by the yellow bicycle's lamp. Old Mr McGregor wore a flat cap and wax jacket.

"Mr McGregor, what are you doing out here?"

"How was yer stay at the wee old place? I hope ye've kept her as ye left her." He took another step into the light. The expression on his face was odd, somewhere between a grimace and a smile. One of his eyes was closed.

No not closed.

Green fuzz covered half of Mr McGregor's face. Some of his teeth were missing. His right hand dangled beside his knee, far too low. His fingers were splayed to make way for a bony talon.

Ryan threw out an arm. "Aaron, get back!"

"He's infected. How?"

"He must have been coming to check on us."

Mr McGregor shambled towards them, arms out like he wanted a hug. Ryan shouted at him to stay back, but the old man didn't listen. He kept coming towards them, determined to make contact.

He's trying to infect us.

Ryan moved left while Aaron moved right. With his attention divided, McGregor looked back and forth between the two brothers. "Hope there's nee mess," he said. "Hope yee bonny lads behaved yeself."

"The party got a little crazy," said Ryan. "Perhaps you should head up there and check the old place out."

"Aye, later for that, lad. First, I just wannee shake yer hand."

Ryan backed away, nearing the opposite edge of the road. From the look of the old landlord, the infection had only just begun to change him. How long had it taken with Brett? Sean had infected him many hours before he had started showing symptoms – almost a full day. Had Mr McGregor been out here all weekend? Had his car died on the road like Tom's?

"Come here, lad." McGregor lunged, swiping his sinewy, too-long arm at Ryan's face. Ryan dodged backwards and his ankle buckled, his left foot coming down on uneven ground. He cried out in shock and pain, then before he knew it, he was falling backwards into the weeds. The back of his skull stuck a patch of rocks and his vision filled with twinkling lights that he at first thought were stars in the sky.

"Shit, Ryan!"

Aaron needs to get out of here. He needs to run.

But he won't.

"Aaron, help me!"

McGregor bore down on Ryan, but Aaron was quick to deliver a firm kick to the side of his thigh. It sent the old man staggering sideways, and allowed enough time for Ryan to clamber to his feet. He was dizzy, and the back of his head felt wet. A wave of nausea took hold of him. He wanted to defend his little brother, but he couldn't. Every time he tried to take a step forward, he went sideways. Every time he tried to reach out, his arms disobeyed him.

McGregor regained his balance and chased after Aaron, both arms swiping at the air. Somewhere nearby an owl hooted. Aaron hopped back and forth, avoiding his attacker with ease. Every now and then he would throw a kick and strike a kneecap or a thigh. Before long, McGregor was limping and stumbling around like the injured old man he was. Bizarrely, though, he didn't grow angry or annoyed. He just kept trying to grab Aaron, methodical and undeterred. Single-minded.

Ryan tried to get a grip of himself. If his brother tripped or made a mistake... If McGregor got his fungus-covered hands on him...

Aaron backed up towards the Land Rover, and when he bumped against it, it startled him and caused him to half turn around. That was all McGregor needed. He leapt at Aaron. Aaron dodged and rolled along the side of the vehicle, just managing to get out of harm's way.

Ryan hurried forward unsteadily and managed to shove the old man in the back. The driver's door was still open and McGregor went sprawling across the seat. There was a loud *clunk* and the Land Rover lurched backwards, the parking brake coming loose. The wheels rolled half a metre, stopping at the edge of a steep ditch bordering the road.

McGregor clambered back out of the Land Rover and tried to grab Ryan again. Ryan tried to escape, but the old man's hand caught his jacket and held on with surprising strength. At the same time, his other hand rose into the air, a talon bursting through sinewy flesh. Any second and it would whip against Ryan's flesh, infecting him.

Ryan screamed in terror and threw himself at McGregor, desperate to do anything that would stop him from whipping that deadly talon. They stumbled on the uneven ground, collided with the back of the Land Rover, and then went pirouetting into the ditch. Ryan slipped, his knee hitting against a rock. It filled him with pain he could barely believe. They tumbled into the ditch, landing awkwardly at the bottom. McGregor's neck twisted beneath him, making a noise like snapping twigs. Ryan thought the old man was dead, but then he began to shuffle around in the weeds, searching. When his fuzzy green eye found Ryan, he crawled towards him, his head hanging at a horrifying angle.

Ryan's leg trembled uncontrollably, the blow to his knee sending his nerve endings into a frenzy. He wanted to stand up and run, but it was impossible. He could only drag himself along the ditch in the same way the old man was doing.

From the road, Aaron called out, "Ryan! Ryan, are you okay? I can't see you down there."

"You need to get out of here— No, wait! The car. Push the car into the ditch."

"What?"

"Push the car backwards. Do it now, Aaron!"

He heard no reply from his little brother, so all Ryan could do was keep crawling away as quickly as he could. McGregor was slower than him, his broken neck causing his gaze to float all over the place and mess up his direction. But Ryan was hurt, and every second it got harder and harder to move. He could feel his knee swelling up.

There was the sound of crunching gravel above.

Ryan looked up and saw the rear of the Land Rover moving more and more into view. It was a heavy vehicle, but Aaron was managing to roll it towards the ditch.

Because he knows my life is at stake.

He's got my back.

I need to get the hell out of the way.

The Land Rover's rear wheels passed over the edge of the embankment and gravity took over. The boxy vehicle seemed to hang in the air for a split second – like the Oblivion ride that had prompted his proposal to Sophie – but then it picked up speed. Ryan scrambled along the ditch, knowing he had a single second before he was crushed to death. His fingers grabbed hold of clumps of grass and weeds as he frantically summoned everything he had left and pulled himself along. McGregor was right behind him, reaching out with his elongated arm, trying to slice Ryan's legs with his talon.

I'm sorry, old man.

The Land Rover crashed into the ditch like a charging rhino, the rear bumper striking the earth and causing the whole vehicle to leap up on its axles. The driver's door slammed shut and the rear bodywork crumpled a little, but the Land Rover was a tank. It came to a stop, barely in any worse shape than it had been before.

McGregor snatched at Ryan's ankle, that deadly talon only inches away from Ryan's flesh, but his arm landed harmlessly in the mud. His head rose up on a broken neck and he seemed to stare pitifully for a moment. Then his fuzzy green eye erupted into a brown mess. His remaining human eye had bulged to the point where it was almost hanging out. Red and green blood spilled from his open mouth.

Ryan shuffled backwards and waited for McGregor to die. It only took a few seconds. Then he reached into his pocket and tossed the old man the keys to the cottage. "I'm checking out, and you can keep my security deposit."

"Ryan? Ryan, are you all right?"

Ryan glanced up the embankment and saw the spectre of his brother standing on the road. The sight of him was a cause to smile. "Yeah, little brother, I'm alive. Help me out of this ditch."

CHAPTER ELEVEN

The journey back to the village was taking longer than expected, mainly because the narrow country road didn't follow a straight line. Instead, it cut back and forth through the rock and hillsides, and while the village might have been two miles away on a Google map, the road could easily have been twice as long. They covered some of the distance by bicycle, but after a while they had decided it would be safer to walk. Ryan's right knee was stiff and he could no longer bend it. It caused him to waddle along like a peg-legged pirate. Despite that, he enjoyed the walk. The fresh air was rejuvenating and the view was comforting. There was nothing and no one around. The infection had ended with poor Mr McGregor. Ryan hadn't known the old man, and yet he felt saddened by his death. Like Brett, Sean, and Loobey, he hadn't deserved to die.

If I hadn't been so desperate to relive the 'glory days', they would still be alive. I dragged everyone out here, hundreds of miles from their lives, because I was scared to marry Sophie. Now there's nothing else I would rather do but hold her in my arms and never let go. She's the best thing that's ever happened to me and I've been too fucking immature to see it. I thought marriage was the end of my life, but it's not. It's the beginning.

I've made a mess of everything.

"Aaron?"

"Yeah?"

"I'm sorry if you felt I was running out on you. The truth is that you're the most important thing in the world to me, and I shouldn't have given you shit about growing up. We're different, and that's okay. I would rather you keep being you than be anything like me. You're a man. A good one."

Aaron looked away, cleared his throat, then said, "You and Sophie are going to have a great life. I'm sorry I've been so stroppy about it all."

"Forgive and forget, man. By the time this shit is over, I imagine we'll be sick to death of each other. I have a feeling it's going to be a while before we get to go back to our normal lives."

"Maybe that's not such a bad thing. I need to get out more. If this weekend has taught me anything, it's that life is too short to slob around indoors all the time."

Ryan smiled. "There's a bright future ahead of you, little brother. I'm glad you finally see that."

"I just wish the past weren't so dark."

"Yeah."

They walked in silence for another thirty minutes, and when Ryan next checked his watch it was almost ten, which was good and bad. Good, because they wouldn't have to reveal their far-fetched nightmare to a bunch of incredulous spectators, but bad because it meant that people would no doubt be dragged from their beds to come and take statements long into the night. Ryan was exhausted, but it would be a while before he saw a bed.

"I think that's the village up ahead," said Aaron, pointing, and when they spotted a 'Welcome' sign, it became certain.

Ryan sighed a breath of relief. "Thank God. Any more walking and my leg's gonna fall off."

The first building they encountered was a bowls club. It had a white-painted woodcutting of a man rolling a ball affixed to the grey stone walls. There was a small, glass-sided tea room adjoining the main building, but the entire place was dark and uninhabited.

"Where do we go?" asked Aaron. "I doubt there's a police station here."

"We'll try the pub in the middle of the village where we parked up. Last orders wouldn't have been very long ago. Any luck and there'll be someone about. We'll head there and call the police."

"Do you think we'll get in trouble for what happened? We should never have messed with that weird corkscrew. We were stupid."

Ryan huffed. "That's an understatement, but it wasn't a crime. How could we have known any of what happened?"

"I suppose you're right. We're never going to get over this, are we? It's not like we'll ever be able to forget or laugh about it."

Ryan stopped walking and stood with his bicycle. He looked at his brother. "Hey, listen to me, okay? Whatever comes next isn't going to be nice or easy, but no matter what, we'll have each other. You and me are alive, and that's all that matters. We're not going to waste a single day looking back and being afraid. I got you, little brother. Everything will sort itself out, okay?"

"Okay."

They left the bowls club behind them and headed for the next set of buildings. A church sat on a low rise to the right, surrounded by a stone wall, and rows upon rows of gravestones. If memory served Ryan correctly, there should be a post office and a row of cottages just beyond. The pub was still a ways off, but no more than a few hundred metres.

The silent walk reminded Ryan of his nights on the town with the lads. Too broke to hire a taxi, they would walk home drunkenly, two or three miles at a time. They would laugh and holler while the rest of the world slept and the highways lay empty. It would have been a happy memory, but things were different now. After the events of the last two days, Ryan looked back now and saw only emptiness and loneliness. The past was gone, curled inwards like paper over a flame. The only way to keep from being consumed by the past was to run towards the future, arms wide open.

I'm ready to run. I'm ready to leave the past behind.

"It's dark," said Aaron, looking around as they walked slowly down the centre of the road. "Quiet."

"It's the middle of the night."

Aaron shook his head. "No, I mean all of the lamp posts are switched off. None of the houses have their lights on. You'd think at least one would have left on a landing light, or a bathroom. There're no lights anywhere. Look around."

Ryan squinted, staring down the cobbled road toward the

village's various buildings. Rows of cottages lined both sides of the road, featureless grey shapes in the moonlight. There was something else too. Something...

"Something's wrong."

Aaron nodded. "I know. What is it?"

"I don't know."

The shadows moved.

Aaron edged closer to Ryan, and Ryan instinctively put an arm around his younger brother. "Don't move. Stay here, right next to me."

Aaron let out a weary sigh, like a part of his soul was leaking out. "I'm so tired, Ryan. I just want to go home."

"Me too." Ryan glanced around, alert, worried. Afraid.

Stomach acids rose into his throat. His guts were trying to tell him something. They were trying to tell him that the weekend wasn't over – and that home was still far away.

"Ryan!" someone shouted. Not Aaron. "My word, I can't believe it!"

Ryan looked towards the church on the right side of the road and spotted a group of people standing inside a porch with glowing candles in their hands. While it was too dark to make out their faces, the person who had shouted was unmistakably familiar – the posh accent especially so. "Tom? Is-Is that you?"

"Yes! Now get inside quickly – and for heaven's sake, hurry."

Aaron tugged at Ryan's arm, pointed to the side of the road. "Look!"

At first it was unclear what Aaron was indicating, but then Ryan's eyes adjusted enough to discern a dim silhouette of a corkscrew.

No.

His eyes flicked to the right, and he spotted a second corkscrew, further away but easy to see due to the way its metallic surface caught and reflected the moonlight.

No!

A wheelie bin toppled over nearby. A creature emerged, formerly human, now waving a pair of talon-tipped tendrils instead of arms.

"Get inside!" Tom cried out. Three more infected people emerged from the shadowy side streets.

"What's going on?" Aaron cried, holding his head like he had flies buzzing inside his skull. "This can't be happening. I don't understand."

"People are sick," shouted Tom, stepping out of the church's porch. "They're *all* sick."

Ryan couldn't move. His mind was cartwheeling down a steep hill, thoughts flying out in all directions as he tried to make sense of what was happening. "Th-The corkscrews, they landed everywhere. It wasn't just the one we found."

Aaron was muttering to himself, still clutching his head and now pulling at his hair. All of his resolve had melted away in an instant. He was a helpless kid again.

The infected people stumbled closer.

Ryan managed to shake himself free of his stupor and grabbed his brother. "Aaron, snap out of it. We have to move."

Aaron blinked twice, let go of his hair, and nodded. "Yeah. Okay."

The Cartwright brother raced towards the church. The whole time, Ryan couldn't help screaming madly inside his own head – *The corkscrews landed everywhere.*

Everywhere.

CHAPTER TWELVE

There had been only darkness, but then came the light. Dim at first, but slowly spreading wide and bright like the petals of a tulip, it cut through the shadows and illuminated metal edges and splintered wood. For a moment, Loobey didn't know where he was. Then, he thought that maybe he was in a prison cell, staring up at a ceiling that was far too low. If not for all the wood, he might have continued down that line of thought, but then he realised he was lying on his back inside a shed. His mind took him no further than that for a moment, but then he remembered it all.

Ryan's stag do.

The cottage.

The fungus.

Shit!

Loobey bolted upright, hitting his shoulder on the underside of an old workbench. He was surrounded by tools and junk. Beside the workbench, a petrol mower hung from a hook. Dust swirled in the shafts of light spilling in through the shed's single window. Hundreds of tiny bugs skittered along the floorboards.

Loobey yelped and dragged himself back along the floor. His hand hit something warm and wet, and when he turned, he saw Sean.

Or what was left of him.

The twisted creature held only scraps of Loobey's former

friend. Pieces of skin here, a patch of ginger hair there. Mostly it was a mass of brown fluids and green fungus, along with the bony carapaces that seemed to grow at random. A pair of metal shears stuck out of Sean's skull, lodged inside his left eye socket. The memory of having put them there flashed through Loobey's weary mind.

I killed Sean. No, the fungus killed Sean. I just dealt with what was left.

Loobey remembered being in the dark with a silent monster whipping at him with two vicious talons. He looked down at his arms now and saw the deep lacerations he had sustained. Dry blood ran from his hands to his elbows.

When he had pulled Sean into the shed with him, it had been an attempt at euthanasia. His death had been certain, but at least he would give Ryan and Aaron a chance to get away. Instead of slowly dying in a bed on a cancer ward, months from now, he had got the chance to die for a reason.

But I ain't dead.

Why ain't I dead?

Loobey reached out and kicked at Sean's corpse, wanting to make sure it wasn't going to suddenly leap up. The fungus had turned Sean into a monster. Who was to say the monster couldn't come back from the dead?

The corpse moved, and Loobey yelped, but the monster was most definitely dead. The movement came from something else.

Bugs.

Sean's remains were infested with four-legged bugs, the same ones that covered the shed floor in their hundreds. Loobey made up his mind to get moving, so he leapt to his feet, surprised at his own agility. For months, he had felt weak and... *heavy.* Now he felt rested, almost excited. Adrenaline coursed through his veins and made him feel connected to every part of his body.

My body. It's still my body.

Loobey looked down at the gash on the back of his right hand. He had got it outside when he had been wrestling with Sean. A talon had bit into his flesh and infected him. The wound had been laced with green oil and subtle strands of green fuzz, and as he looked at it now, he still saw the fungus, but it had blackened. The fungus had spread no further than his hand. How long had the infection taken with Brett and Sean?

Sean was covered in the stuff after a few hours. Brett changed in less than a day. How long have I been lying here?

Loobey stared out of the window. It was made from a sheet of murky plastic, so the only thing he could see was that it was daylight. When Ryan and Aaron had escaped on the bikes, it had been evening – not even midnight.

I've been lying here for hours. After I planted the shears in Sean's skull, I... I lost my breath and passed out. I was exhausted. It was too much.

But now I feel... okay. I feel better than I have in months.

Loobey felt like he was trapped inside a dream, confused by the strange logic of an imagined world. As much as he felt in touch with his own body, he felt completely adrift from reality. Sean was a rotten mess on the floor. Alien bugs swarmed at his feet.

But I feel healthy.

Loobey took a shaky step towards the shed door. It wasn't weakness that caused him to shake, it was energy. He was a bag of nervous electricity. A firework ready to explode.

He shoved open the shed door and leapt into the weak sunshine. The day was cold, but he barely felt it. The blood in his veins ran hot. The colours of the world almost overwhelmed him. The greens, the oranges, the greys. They seemed to shimmer and vibrate, begging for his attention. Only when he focused did the colours remain still. The air was like crisp ice chips in his lungs.

It was only when his gaze fell upon Brett's body, twisted and distorted the same as Sean's, that the euphoria began to fade away. His friends were dead. Brett, Sean, most likely Tom too.

My friends are all dead.

No. Ryan and Aaron got away. They're alive.

I need to find them.

Loobey turned a circle for a moment, finding it hard to put his thoughts in order. He needed to get to the village, but which way was it?

The road. Just follow the road. The road leads to the village.

And people.

Yes, people.

Loobey took the first step, and then he was moving, almost at a jog. His lungs and heart pumped happily, full of vigour. Full of life. He would make it to his destination in no time. But halfway down the hill, toward the stream, Loobey slowed down. A fox stood staring at him, half its face covered by green fuzz. Beside the fox stood a massive brown hare, also partially covered in fuzz. In the distance, an owl hooted – strange for that time of day. The fox and the hare continued eyeing Loobey up for a few more seconds, then they turned away, uninterested.

Loobey let out a sigh of relief and picked up speed again. He didn't know why the animals didn't attack like those inside the cottage, but he wasn't going to complain. Maybe the fungus affected individual animals in different ways.

Ryan and Aaron will get help. We'll figure all this out. Someone will know what's going on. Someone will make all this better.

Loobey started running. He needed to get to the village. He needed to find his friends.

He needed to find *people*.

Don't miss out on your FREE Iain Rob Wright horror pack. Five terrifying books sent straight to your inbox.

No strings attached & signing up is a doddle.

Just visit www.iainrobwright.com

PLEA FROM THE AUTHOR

Hey, Reader. So you got to the end of my book. I hope that means you enjoyed it. Whether or not you did, I would just like to thank you for giving me your valuable time to try and entertain you. I am truly blessed to have such a fulfilling job, but I only have that job because of people like you; people kind enough to give my books a chance and spend their hard-earned money buying them. For that I am eternally grateful.

If you would like to find out more about my other books then please visit my website for full details. You can find it at:

www.iainrobwright.com.

Also feel free to contact me on Facebook, Twitter, or email (all details on the website), as I would love to hear from you.

If you enjoyed this book and would like to help, then you could think about leaving a review on Amazon, Goodreads, or anywhere else that readers visit. The most important part of how well a book sells is how many positive reviews it has, so if you leave me one then you are directly helping me to continue on this journey as a full time writer. Thanks in advance to anyone who does. It means a lot.

MORE HORROR BOOKS BY IAIN ROB WRIGHT

Escape!

Dark Ride

12 Steps

The Room Upstairs

Animal Kingdom

AZ of Horror

Sam

ASBO

The Final Winter

The Housemates

Sea Sick

Ravage

Savage

The Picture Frame

Wings of Sorrow

TAR

House Beneath the Bridge

The Peeling

Blood on the bar

THE HELL ON EARTH SERIES

The Gates (Book 1)

Legion (Book 2)

Extinction (Book 3)

Defiance (Book 4)

Resurgence (Book 5)

Rebirth (Book 6)

Iain Rob Wright is one of the UK's most successful horror and suspense writers, with novels including the critically acclaimed, THE FINAL WINTER; the disturbing bestseller, ASBO; and the wicked screamfest, THE HOUSEMATES.

His work is currently being adapted for graphic novels, audio books, and foreign audiences. He is an active member of the Horror Writer Association and a massive animal lover.

www.iainrobwright.com
FEAR ON EVERY PAGE

For more information
www.iainrobwright.com
iain.robert.wright@hotmail.co.uk

www.ingramcontent.com/pod-product-compliance
Ingram Content Group UK Ltd.
Pitfield, Milton Keynes, MK11 3LW, UK
UKHW031314130125
4087UKWH00042B/252